CLOSER THAN

ENEMIES

2

By

KAREN MARIE COLEMAN

Karen Coleman

ISBN: 978-1-7328314-0-7

Kaldonya Brunson
PUBLISHING

Email <u>authorkarencoleman@yahoo.com</u>

Visit our official Website at: www.karencoleman.org

Table of Contents

Prologue

Dante Castellucci, the founder and president of the Castellucci Corporation/Criminal Organization, has called a brief meeting among associates. The members of the private gathering sought to avoid the prying eyes of the FBI or any other law enforcement agencies trying to spy on their organization, which has been operating stealthily for the past thirty-plus years.

The meeting occurred in a recently renovated mid-rise building in New Jersey. The location was once a busy storefront and apartments. The building was used by the families of the Italian American community when the area was bustling with busy shoppers and street vendors peddling their wares, authentic products that could only be found in their native country. The building had been condemned by the city and was earmarked for demolition to make room for another project. Because of its significance to Dante, his corporation purchased the building and then renovated it, turning it into luxury condos. There are twenty-four units in the entire building. Six of them had outdoor terraces. The largest apartment is used by Dante and his elite group of friends.

This location is where million-dollar deals, murder plots, and other criminal activities had been discussed. The gang has gathered, once again, for another one of those discussions. Dante trusted these men due to their continued loyalty since growing up together on the streets of Hoboken. Although they were his trusted friends, he used many precautions to protect his conversation, including searching, using wireless jammers, and other means in the rare event that either of them would turn on him.

First, Lucio Piazza is Dante's trusted confidant and best friend. They're the same age and the eldest of the group. Their bond goes far beyond friendship. It was more of a brotherhood. Their parents operated businesses out of this very building. Dante's parents owned a grocery store and a small restaurant. Lucio's father ran a bakery next door. The two practically grew up on this street.

A couple of Italian guys from the opposing neighborhood were known for harassing business owners in the area. Among those targeted were Dante's parents, his uncle Micky Castellucci and his wife, who also ran a business in the building, and Lucio's family. These menacing thugs were the Venturi brothers. They extorted money and took valuable items from families who were barely making enough to meet their needs.

One day, Dante's father, Francois Castellucci, had enough and decided he wouldn't pay any more extortion money. Neither was he prepared to give away any more free products. He was tired of his hard-working family taking losses at someone else's hands. He'd instructed his wife to hide the money earlier in the day with the anticipation the thugs would make their usual visit. Sure enough, just like clockwork, they arrived. Francois peered out his store window, watching as the two men went from store to store. He instructed his young son, Dante, to hide in the back with his mother. The men made their way to his brother's store. The exchange was swift as Micky Castellucci didn't want them in his store any longer than needed. He had the money and items already ready for them. Now they were at Francois Castellucci's store. His wife and son never made it to the back of the store.

The large man with a dented scar over his eye was the older of the two brothers. He stood up to the senior Castellucci and placed a knife to his throat. The younger Venturi brother, equally as large and threatening as his brother, was dressed in a dark grey wool suit and wearing a matching fedora, which he undoubtedly had taken from some other poor chap. This guy moved closer to Dante's mother, Rosa. She shrieked at the sound of the switchblade opening. She quickly grabbed young Dante by the arm and pulled him close to her. She watched as they robbed Francois of the few dollars he had in his shirt pocket.

"This can't be all of it. Where's the rest of the money?"

A thud landed in Francois' abdomen.

Seven-year-old Dante clung to his mother's apron as the other brother towered over her with the switchblade still in his hand. He took her arm, pulled her close to him, and asked, "Where's the money?"

"There is no more. That's all we have."

Sandwiched between his mother and the man, young Dante buried his head in his mother's apron and began to cry. He then peeped up at the man again, studying his face, which frightened him. Fire seemed to pour from his bloodshot eyes as he glared at the child. The bell from the entry door jingled. It was a beat cop who'd come in to grab a drink before his daily shift. As he looked around the store for what he needed, the older Venturi brother stared at the couple, daring them to say a word. The cop placed an RC cola on the counter and looked up for assistance. The Venturi brothers noticed the cop had a partner waiting in the car. After not getting what they came for due to the cop's visit, the men stood down. They backed away from the family and left the store, but not before taking a few items.

Dante could never erase the men's faces from his memory. He remembered the pain on his father's face as he was rendered helpless, unable to save his wife from their abuse, and how this broke his father's heart and diminished his pride. Even still, Dante loved and respected his father. What could a man do when he's facing these types of bullies? The people were helpless against these thugs. The extortion and abuse went on for years until Dante and Lucio, who were in their early teens, decided to put a stop to it.

They gained the trust of the Venturi brothers by pretending to submit to them, and they even joined their crew while learning about their daily operations. They plotted the murder of both men. Although they were afraid, they were angered. Since no one in the community would do anything to help, they felt it was their duty to rescue their family from the deadbeats. After the deed was done, the boys seemed to mature. They became well-known as ones not to be trifled with. They protected their community against all bullies. It was their neighborhood, and they staked their claim to that turf. After their first kill, killing became easier for them, thus beginning their life of crime. These two have committed crimes that only they know of, which have gotten them to where they are today.

There was Tommy Moretti, a friend who's proved his loyalty time and time again, even taking a charge for Dante in the early years. He did a small stint in prison so that his friend could maintain a clean criminal record, thereby allowing him to finish college and ultimately become the success he is today.

Then there was Angelo, Nicky, and Benny, Dante's cousins. They, too, carry the Castellucci name. These were Micky's sons. They're the true muscle who carries out Dante's deadly orders. Their parents were killed as a result of a hit from a rival gang. Dante's parents raised the three brothers as their own. They were adamant that the boys get their education. The young teens attended high school by day, but they were committing crimes during the evenings and weekends alongside Dante, Lucio, and Tommy. The Castellucci cousins' first kill, with the help of Dante's gang, involved tracking down those responsible for killing the cousin's parents. The Castellucci crew struck fear in the hearts of other gangs, who'd witnessed the effects of the bloodbath against those who'd dare come against them. They had now become the bullies they'd despised, albeit they wouldn't prey on their own people.

They continued to rule through fear, power, and dominance. They respected and cared for the elderly or poorer families in their neighborhood by donating cash, paying bills, and bringing in gifts from Sicily that many of the elders longed for but couldn't quite afford, thereby purchasing their silence with many gifts and favors.

This group of Italian men had been responsible for all the crimes in that region and beyond since their youth—initially, the bulk of their assets derived from ill-gotten gain.

Dante, obsessed with making money, educated himself in the world of finance by obtaining his

MBA, bachelor's, and master's degree in finance. He ultimately acquired several legitimate businesses. However, there were many rumors that he was the leader of the criminal organization, and rightfully so. He'd convinced everyone, including law enforcement members, that he was a legitimate businessman who gained most of his wealth by making sound investments. He'd illegally boosted his financial portfolio. He began pooling his resources together with high-class investors and other men of wealth making millions. Afterwards, he branched out on his own with a clean financial slate. He was wise enough to know when to escape risky criminal activity, especially when he realized how much money he could make legally. He'd grown tired of the traditional crimes, which were sure to either get him killed or result in lengthy prison sentences for all involved.

Long gone were the days when he and the guys were young thugs shaking down rivals in the old neighborhood. Instead of taking over neighborhoods through turf wars and many crimes, they were now taking over corporations that had fallen on hard times and were forced to sell by buying them at a fraction of their worth.

Dante's corporation was like hungry lions waiting to pounce on its prey, devouring it and picking the carcass clean. His deals whether back-end or legitimate, are now done in fancy boardrooms. That is unless he's planning a murder. Rarely did he use this as an option but when he did, he rationalized it as a necessary evil, but only as a last resort.

With the realization that murders brought heat, there were to be no murders or violence of any form carried out without Dante's approval. He groomed his crew into the world of finance and encouraged them to educate themselves in their respective fields further.

It wasn't long before they, too, had become successful. To the Castellucci organization, the corporate world was no different from that of the streets. The same principle was applied: strong leadership, supply, demand, profit margins, and crushing the competitor.

Dante stood in the corner of the terrace overlooking the Hudson River. With towering height, his regal appearance was that of an important dignitary, with his Italian suit tailor-made to fit him to perfection. The evening sun highlighted the silver tones in his lush, thick, onyx hair. Clean-shaven and handsome, at fifty-seven, he still turned the heads of young and old ladies. Strikingly good looks, coupled with a vast financial portfolio, women flocked to him. Although he was married, it had been a couple of years since anyone had seen him and his wife together in public, sparking rumors that perhaps the couple had called it quits.

He kept his daily exercise regimen with his personal trainer and weekly appointments with his in-house barber and stylists who he kept on the payroll. He was meticulous in his appearance almost to the point of obsession. In doing so, others in the organization felt he was becoming too Americanized. He looked every bit of the distinguished business tycoon, and for all intents and purposes, he was just that.

As a hero to many Italians who felt he was the epitome of an ideal success story by achieving the American dream, their small-time Italian boy had made good in the States. But to those who truly knew him, especially those who'd been negatively impacted by his reign of terror, he was a ruthless killer and shouldn't be crossed in any way.

Aside from his shady deals and dirty money, he owned the controlling shares of an advanced tech company.

A new business venture from a privately held company was in the works. The company was set to go global. Many corporations sought to merge with the company, seeing the millions they were already making, but the group turned down their offers, opting to partner with the Castellucci Corporation. Dante stood to make billions from the merger, which would continue solidifying his place as a well-respected business mogul, placing him on the Forbes list of one of the richest men in America. While he welcomed the thought of being named the most influential and wealthiest man, he would've much rather remained anonymous, but the type of money he was making brought plenty of attention.

Life was going well for Dante, but he was presented with a problem. Several politicians were speaking out against the merger and the money he stood to gain. They began to target him personally, even bringing up the rumors of his possible involvement in organized crime, which infuriated him.

He tried all he could to get them to halt the attacks and their stance on the issue. They were constantly expressing their concerns in the media. They felt that the American people would be at a disadvantage if the companies were allowed to merge. They also feared it would put smaller companies at a disadvantage. After failing to convince them to come aboard, he felt it was time to take other measures. This meeting discussed how and when orders will be carried out to remove them from office by force or, more preferably, by death. Everyone huddled together as Dante Castellucci began to speak.

"Alright, guys. Listen up. We've passed every regulatory hurdle on this MSP Communications deal; now we're just waiting for the Justice Department to approve the merger. While that may sound like wonderful news, we have two annoying problems. The congressman from Texas and the other from Maryland are dead set on stopping this deal. They're gaining a loyal following on the issue. We've tried everything to get them to come aboard, but they're trying to cut their teeth on this deal while making examples of us. These men know nothing about business. They barely know politics. I didn't come this far to be stopped by some cut-rate country bumpkin and some asshole with a high school diploma that was only voted in because his daddy was popular."

His good friend Lucio chimed in,

"So, what do you propose we do? You know we must be careful about this since everyone knows where they stand on the issue. If any harm comes to them, they'll blame you, especially the guy from Texas. He vocally challenged you during his last press conference on Capitol Hill. What was it he said? *I ain't afraid of no mob or Castellucci. He can bring all the men he wants against me, but I'm not going away.*

Our hands are tied. We must allow this thing to play itself out." Shaking his head while looking incredulously, Dante rubbed his fingers under his chin and said, "I don't think so. There are ways around anything; you must know what you're doing. We can conquer them. There are many ways of squashing annoying pests." Still trying to convince his good friend, Lucio moved closer to him. He stood directly in his face as they were the same height. His white hair was slightly mussed, and his clothes were disheveled as he'd dressed hurriedly. He wasn't wearing a tie. He'd napped a little later than he'd planned that evening. With a weathered expression, his reddened eyes met Dante's, pleading with him to take his advice.

"Yeah, but the people trust you. Look at how far you've come, for Christ's sake. You've cleaned up your image. If you move forward with your plan, you'll have nothing to gain, and you could lose everything. You gotta wait this thing out. Anyway, they're just making a bunch of noise. As you said, they're trying to cut their teeth on this deal. They're securing votes for themselves for the next election. It's all about politics. They're speaking too little too late. Everyone knows this deal is going to go through. Stop worrying."

Dante walked around in circles with his hands folded behind his back. He stopped and let out a deep sigh. "I suppose you're right, Lou. I guess I'll busy myself with other matters until we're approved.

He directed his attention toward Nicky, Benny, and Angelo and said,

"Boys, I need you to think of something. Be clever, and don't make a move until I say so. Lou, I had you scheduled to meet with the heads of the company in Maine, but I'm going to need you and Tommy to stay here in town. We have a few meetings to attend concerning the property over in Statin Island. I'm thinking about selling it. We've milked it for all it's worth. I think it's time to let go of it now. That'll free up some cash for the Maine properties."

"Alright, Castellucci, I'm going to stay here. Just call me when you need me, Lucio said.

"I'll be right here," said Tommy.

Angelo, the oldest of the cousins, responded,

"If you need us, we're here. Just stay calm and focused. Remember, we don't have to harm anyone physically; we can kill them professionally. What we've got planned for them, they're going to wish they were dead. The scandal will be one for the ages. They may even get a little prison time, just as we did with Senator Willis. Just give us the word."

Benny, Dante's youngest cousin, was standing to his right. Dante looked down on his petite frame as he agreed with Angelo.

"Boss," he said, getting ready to light his cigar.

"We'll handle things from here."

Although Benny was small at just under five feet, he was quite deadly, especially toward those who thought they'd bully him because of his size. He lit his cigar. After taking a large puff, the wind carried the cloud of smoke upwards towards Dante's face, burning his eyes and filling his nostrils with smoke. His nose wrinkled as he leaned backwards to fan the air.

"Hey Benny, what in the hell did I tell you about smoking around me? Are you trying to kill me or what? Do you know that over fifty-thousand people die every year from second-hand smoke?"

Benny snuffed the cigar out on the metal railing, and they were standing near the edge of the terrace. "Sorry, Dante. It won't happen again." Lucio, looking on, chuckled and shook his head.

"Look at you, Dante. You've become so Americanized that you've even lost your accent. You sound like one of d'em commercials. *Over fifty-thousand people die every year from secondhand smoke*," he said mockingly.

"You're lucky I love you like a brother. I'd normally have a guy whacked for fucking with me. But hey, what's wrong with a fella wanting to take care of his body? If you eat right, exercise, and stop putting all kinds of toxins in your body, you'll be healthy, and you won't look old before your time. Take you, for instance, Lou; we're the same age, but you look like you're in your seventies. You can barely walk up a flight of stairs without oxygen. You love chasing younger women, but you can't even keep up with them. After you're done sleeping with them; or should I say after they're done with you, you sleep half the day away. You got no energy or stamina. Those young women are gonna be the death of you. I swear you're gonna die right on top of one of'em, you mark my words. And the rest of you boys are aging like bananas. You eat anything you want. You smoke and drink heavily, and you don't exercise. Because I choose to take care of myself, you say I'm Americanized. No, I'm smart. I want to live a long healthy life. I want to be around to enjoy my wealth. As far as me hanging around with other wealthy Americans; I mix and mingle in all the right circles. I keep my hands clean and because of that, we can make all the money we want. Not to mention the fact that I've gained the respect and admiration of corporate America. I've been featured in countless magazines and hundreds of articles in print. Due to my ability to see the value in certain stocks, and pick my business ventures wisely, the world of finance seeks my advice on such matters. They're throwing out words like a *brilliant* and *wise businessman.* Of course, the five of us understand what we do beneath the surface. We must protect our image. Image is everything. As Italians, we're already a stereotype. I don't want to be known as some dangerous mob boss. That's why I expressed that we handle ourselves accordingly while blending in with the rest of corporate America. As a result, you guys have profited greatly under my leadership. We're practically legitimate. So, stop busting my balls about this Americanized foolishness, and start taking care of your bodies. You'll look and feel better, although there may not be any hope for you Cousin Benny."

The men chatted a little more while leaving the terrace. The cousins escorted Dante to his vehicle.

Dante got in the back seat of his car. His driver looked in the rear-view mirror and said,

"While you were inside, Mrs. Castellucci called. She asked me to bring you home right away, sir. She says she has something special planned. How do you want me to proceed?"

Dante exhaled. He was in no way prepared to spend the evening with his wife. Dante had been one of the wealthiest eligible bachelors until around the age of thirty-eight years old. That's when he met and married a nineteen-year-old A-list Italian actress. For years they'd been the talk in Hollywood, and elite circles. Salacious stories of the rumored mob boss and his sexy young actress, made for juicy headlines not only in America but abroad. Their love fascinated the world, and they appeared to be joined at the hip. Fans were fascinated with how she could get one of America's most eligible bachelors to not only fall in love with her but also manage to get him to shed his bad-boy ways, albeit he denied any involvement in the criminal underworld. When she was away filming, he would be flown in by private jet to her location.

He funded many of her films and lent money to major studios to ensure her projects were successful. She was it. Their love was strong, but lately, they'd been going through some personal trials, and Dante didn't want to deal with the issues in their marriage. He'd deliberately turned his cell phone off so his wife couldn't contact him. He sat staring out the window, contemplating his next move. The driver slowed down his speed. After a few minutes of not getting an answer, he pulled over.

"Giovanni, take me to the penthouse on fifty-seventh. I have another meeting. Tell her it'll have to wait until tomorrow if she calls again. I'm busy tonight."

The driver slowly pulled away from the curb and proceeded to his destination. He pulled up to the building and Dante exited the vehicle and made his way to the entrance.

"Good evening, Mr. Castellucci," the doorman said, greeting him with a friendly smile. Dante nodded his head as he went inside. He had a lot on his mind. He was still nervous about the merger, and he couldn't seem to relax until he knew he had sealed the deal. He was glad he was able to elude his wife. Now, all he needed was a drink, a light dinner, and some rest.

When he exited the elevator, aromatic notes of Italian cuisine permeated the air. As he walked in the door of the penthouse, he smiled as the smell wafted across his nostrils. "Ahhh, just in time for dinner," he said under his breath. Normally his house attendant Genovese, would meet him at the door, take his jacket, and hand him his drink. He'd forgiven her for not being there, as he was happy she was making a great meal. He made his way to the wet bar to fix a scotch and soda. The clanging of pots and pans made him wonder what was being prepared. He was ready for a sample of whatever was being cooked, just to tide him over until dinner time. He made his way into the kitchen.

"Genovese," he said, calling out to her.

"I gave her the night off," his wife said in an abrupt tone. She was standing at the stove barefoot with an apron on. Her back was to him.

"Happy anniversary, love," she said, smiling. His shoulders slumped; he let out a burst of air. He leaned back on the counter and rubbed the back of his neck with his right hand while his left gripped the glass of scotch. She turned towards him and said,

"Taste this Saltimbocca. It's your favorite from my Nonna's recipe. The veal is very fresh. The prosciutto is nice and salty, and I added extra fresh mozzarella just like you like it." As she placed the fork to his mouth, he firmly pressed his lips together, slightly turned his head, and refused the food.

"I'm not hungry. I've already eaten."

"Well, that's never stopped you before. Go on, taste it." Showing no interest, he averted his eyes, not wanting to make eye contact.

"Delilah dear, what're you doing here? I thought you were home?"

"I *was* home, but after I hadn't heard from you, I figured you'd be here. I get tired of sitting in that house all cooped up. Day in and day out, I sit alone. As a married woman, I spend a lot of my days alone. You don't take me out and rarely spend time with me. I feel as though we're drifting apart. We used to be so in love. Now, I only see you in passing. I was thinking perhaps we could take a trip together, you know, renew our vows or go on another couple's retreat. After all, it is our anniversary."

"I can't leave now; I have too many irons in the fire. I have this merger, not to mention other important deals. I must be in New York just in case we're called to sign off on these contracts. I can't just pick up and leave the city. It would be a bad move."

She tried to remain calm as he gave yet another excuse, one of many he's given over the past couple of years. She placed the fork on the stove, untied her apron, and laid it on the counter. She walked closer to him. She tried to cozy up to him and kissed him underneath his chin.

"Not now," he said as he gently pushed her away. He made his way into the bedroom, hoping she wouldn't follow, but he knew she would. He felt a sense of guilt for not being able to respond to her in the manner she deserved. This was one of many awkward moments he'd tried to avoid.

He loosened his tie and made a quick escape into the walk-in closet. He placed the tie with the others and removed his suit jacket. She was unrelenting. She cornered him in the closet before he could re-enter the bedroom. He had no choice but to interact with her. Again, she stood before him, hoping for some compassion, but she was met with coldness of heart, and it was breaking her.

"I love you, Dante. Please tell me you still love me," she pleaded

"Let's not do this tonight. I have a lot on my mind. I can't take you doing this again."

"Look at me, Dante," she said, holding back the tears. He couldn't bring himself to look at her. He looked past her, staring into nothingness.

"Why won't you look at me?" she shouted out of frustration. "You promised me. You promised that our love would never change." He gritted his teeth, trying not to respond as he didn't want to cause her any more pain. She kept up the pressure. Finally, he said,

"What do you want from me, Delilah?"

"I'm your wife. I need you to love me, hold me like you used to. Let me feel the warmth of your arms around me as you love my body with all the passion of two young lovers. Like old times. Don't treat me as if I'm a stranger. Stop making excuses each time we make plans. The feelings of abandonment and neglect have me dying inside. I don't have friends anymore. The ladies have stopped inviting me to their gatherings. If it weren't for my mother, I'd have nobody. Everyone has abandoned me including you."

Dante turned towards her and yelled,

"Delilah, I didn't do this. You did! Everything was perfect. You were perfect then you had to go and ruin things."

"But, I did it for you!"

"No, you did it for yourself. If you had listened to me things would be different. Now you try to force me to see things your way. I told you to give me some time to get used to the way things are now. You keep pushing me, and it's pushing me farther away."

"That's because I need you, Dante. I have nowhere else to turn."

Tears formed in her eyes. "I need you. I've been forced to face this alone." She was used to her husband doting on her. Since her father died when she was thirteen, he was more than just her husband; he was like a father figure to her. Whenever she was in trouble, he came to her rescue. He tutored her in just about everything. He encouraged her to finish college and taught her about the world of finance. Anything she wanted to know, he was there to give her the answers. He even helped her in business, taking her earnings from her film career and investing them for her. She was the youngest and wealthiest movie starlet in the history of America. He was her biggest fan, advocate, and fierce protector. She hung on to every word that came from his mouth. She worshipped him. Having his love and approval meant everything. It was difficult for her to fathom the treatment he was now giving her, and she was unable to properly process what was happening to her.

In her desperate attempt to get his attention, she reached around his waist, holding him tight. He didn't want to hurt her, but he didn't want to lead her on either. He reluctantly wrapped his arms around her. He didn't say a word. His awkward silence spoke volumes.

From the moment he looked at her, her youthful beauty, alluring charm, innocence, and vibrant spirit appealed to him. She'd begun to mature from a child actor to a budding Hollywood starlet. She was the latest buzz, and her star was rising fast. Not to mention, as a young woman, she was at the height of her sexuality, and she loved their lovemaking as he was experienced and seemed to know everything about pleasing the female body. He had to make her his. He was obsessed with her love. They were joined at the hip. Things are different now. She reasoned within that if given a little time, he'd come around. She would at least try once more to regain his affection, but at that moment, she could tell his feelings had truly changed. He was responding out of pity, which intensified her pain. She didn't want his pity. This moment was far worse than all the rejections she'd experienced.

Trying to salvage what was left of her pride, she lifted her head from his shoulders and pushed away. With tears in her eyes, she said,

"Perhaps I shouldn't have come." She turned on her heels and entered the other room to get her things. He watched as she slipped her shoes on.

She reached for her purse and began walking towards the door.

"Wait; you don't have to leave," he said. You can stay. After all, you're still my wife."

She looked over her shoulder and said,

"Thank you, love. You've almost convinced me of your sincerity, but I know better. I'm going home. I'll be there until you decide on your next move. I'll give you all the time and space you need." She placed her purse on her shoulder, put on her shades and head scarf, and began leaving. To clear his conscience, he said,

"For what it's worth, I've never been unfaithful." Although the statement meant everything to him, and it *was* indeed true, she wasn't moved by the confession. Dante's father was a faithful man. He taught his son what it meant to be faithful. He wanted so badly to pattern his life after his father. While he held dear the principles his dad taught him, he knew principles barely kept food on the table, good food that was. He watched his parents struggle to raise him and his cousins after their parents died, and he admired the love they shared. They weren't rich, but they enjoyed life. Dante felt his parents deserved the best for their many sacrifices, and he took care of them until they died. When he met his wife, he wanted to be every bit the husband to Delilah as his father was to his mother. He wanted his wife to understand what that statement truly meant to him. Aside from his mother, she was the pride of his life, and he loved having her on his arm. They were the perfect couple, but things were different now, and he was devastated. Not knowing how to convey his feelings, he came off as callous and unsympathetic while trying to cope with their dilemma. She ignored his comment and continued on her way, leaving him with a myriad of feelings.

Dante Castellucci, one of the most powerful and feared men, cowered to his younger wife, hanging his head in shame. He made a promise to love her for eternity. He was aware of her pain. Due to her visit, he was forced to confront emotions that had lain dormant for the past two years, yet he still needed more time to get used to their new normal.

CHAPTER ONE

After an exhausting night of caring for a fussy baby, Peyton was finally able to enjoy some much-needed time for herself. As she stepped into the steam shower, the stresses from the hectic night rolled off her shoulders. She found the hot water refreshing and soothing to her tired body. She had just begun to lather herself when the sounds of her baby's cries coming from the baby monitor interrupted her moment of solitude. "Aww, come on, Gracie. Give mommy a break," she said, exhaling.

She didn't bother rinsing. Instead, she frantically searched for her robe. She quickly exited the shower, almost tripping on the bathmat. The crying suddenly stopped.

"I've got her babe!"

She let out a sigh of relief as her husband's voice came over the baby monitor. She was able to finish her shower. Afterwards, she went into the nursery to relieve him. For the most part, Peyton chose to care for her baby herself, especially since she'd chosen to breastfeed. They employed a full-time nanny to assist her, in the event Peyton would fill in for her father at his law firm. Gil was standing fully dressed for work in his professional attire. Wearing a neatly pressed lavender shirt, with eggplant colored tie, and gray slacks. The proud doting father donned a gentle smile with a perfectly trimmed goatee. His naturally wavy hair was cut low. He was rocking, and calming the baby, lulling her back to sleep. He enjoyed relieving his wife so he could spend more time with the baby. The picturesque scene of father and daughter reminded Peyton of her own father. She couldn't help but wonder had her dad held and loved her with as much love as Gil did their daughter. She was proud of her husband for tackling fatherhood with such eagerness. She smiled warmly at Gil, then slowly batted her eyes in a thankful motion. She was still in her robe. It was feeding time.

"Come to mommy sweetie," she said while motioning for Gil to hand her the baby. She made herself comfortable in the large, plush rocking recliner, and began to nurse. With adoration, he looked on as she nursed. Her curly hair was atop her head in a loose ponytail. A few curly strands ran down the side of her smooth honey-colored face. Every few seconds, their eyes met. He wanted to participate in every aspect of their daughter's care, from feedings to just giving her the love and care she needed.

Gil and Peyton are first-time parents. Gil is in his early forties, and Peyton is in her late thirties. They'd never really discussed having children. They were both enjoying their lives, careers, and the vast wealth they'd amassed due to their hard work and sound investments. It wasn't until Peyton became pregnant that the prospect of having a child came to light. Nevertheless, the pregnancy was a very welcome surprise.

Although they were first-time parents, Gil wasn't surprised at how well Peyton transitioned into motherhood. She'd always been caring and nurturing. She loved children. Almost every aspect of her benevolence was geared toward the youth and the less fortunate in their community. Although eager to be a father, Gil wasn't sure how well he would fare in the role of fatherhood. He was eager to find out. Armed with the wisdom of their parents, parenting classes, and child-rearing books, as well as a live-in nanny, calmed his fears.

"I knew you would be a great mother," he said. "You're such a natural at it. Hell, I still get nervous when I hold her. She's so fragile. I'm afraid I'll break her."

"Oh, Gil; you're an awesome father. She adores you. You can see how she's comforted each time you hold her."

"I sure hope so. I love her, and you, my love; you've given me over seventeen years of a wonderful marriage and finally a beautiful baby girl. My life is fulfilled. I never knew what I was missing until the Lord blessed me with you, and now, our little Grace."

Gil leaned in and kissed Peyton's forehead, then his daughter's. A male's voice over the intercom interrupted the intimate moment.

"Mr. Wilkes, the car is ready." Gil wanted to spend more time with his family. He'd already taken paternity leave during the first six weeks of the baby's arrival, and although she was now four months old, he still found it difficult to leave her. He was needed at his practice due to a backlog of clients, who'd refused to have anyone other than Gil perform their surgeries. They postponed their procedures, opting to wait until his family leave was over. He was finally getting back into a routine, and his schedule was back at a steady pace. He kissed his wife one last time and said to the man listening on the other end of the intercom,

"Mr. Sam, I'm on my way."

Samuel R. Banks is Gil's personal caregiver. He's an older gentleman in his mid-sixties. He was hired as a favor to Peyton's father. He was a loyal God-fearing man, more of a grandfatherly figure. He's a Memphis native. He and his wife of forty-two years raised two sons, Samuel Jr. and Elijah, plus a daughter, Pamela. They live in New Orleans, Louisiana where his wife is originally from. After his wife passed, his children tried to get him to move with them, but he declined. He loved his children, but he wouldn't think of leaving his home, a place that he'd built from the ground up, a home that he and his wife made for themselves and their children. His fondest memories of his lovely wife and children kept him alive. He lived an active lifestyle by playing tennis and golf, and he volunteered at the elementary school, reading to preschoolers and kindergarteners. His animated style of storytelling drew the children and staff to him. There, he was affectionately known as, Grandpa Banks.

Samuel retired from the service industry, where Peyton's father, Henry Brockington, a prominent attorney, befriended him at the local country club. Mr. Brockington was one of the few black members, so Mr. Samuel took extra special care of him. He was nearing retirement, but he still wanted to work part-time.

The Wilkes were looking to hire an assistant who would be able to tend to Gil's needs. So, Peyton's father recommended Mr. Samuel for the position. He's worked as a steward for the family for over twelve years. His main duty was taking care of Gil, but over the years, he took on more tasks by helping the family anywhere he felt he was needed. He was a welcome presence for the couple, and they'd grown to love him. They received him as a member of their family. Being around them reminded him of his own family, and it allowed him to do what he enjoyed. That was caring for others. The job wasn't simply about the money. He had a small nest egg in his savings as well as the money from his wife's life insurance policy. He was saving it for his grandchildren's future, with the hopes his children would produce them. He was great friends with the Wilkes and the Brockington family. He took pride in his work, and he'd never missed a day of his twelve years of employment.

Mr. Samuel's seen his fair share of scandals during his years of employment in the service industry. He'd been exposed to many secrets. Secrets that to this day have never been uttered from his lips. No one had to force a non-disclosure agreement on him. He ensured the privacy of his employers by not once ever betraying their trust. Although there were very few scandals within the Wilkes household, there was a time recently when the couple's marriage was on the rocks due to an unfortunate incident. Peyton's former best friend had set out to destroy her marriage which resulted in a brief separation between the couple. After her plan was exposed, Gil and Peyton reconciled. They renewed their vows and they're happier and more in love than ever. Mr. Samuel witnessed the separation of the couple he'd come to love as his own children. He kept the faith, knowing that their love for God and one another would persevere. He was thrilled when they reconciled.

There was another reason he enjoyed coming to work: Silvia McClain, the Wilke's beautiful chef and house steward. Silvia was the same age as Samuel. She was a plump lady around two-hundred and fifty-five pounds. She was very shapely for her size, something Samuel really loved about her. She had fair skin and long gray hair. She was a jovial, kind-hearted friend who cared about everyone, including Samuel. Silvia was a great cook. She'd operated her own restaurant, which was handed down to her by her parents, with great success. The soul food restaurant, which had been in business for over forty-five years, was named after Silvia by her parents as she was their only child. She took over the business when her parents retired and kept it going for twenty-five of those years. After a while, she made the difficult decision to sell the popular eatery. The community expressed their sadness over the issue. The restaurant was a staple in the community. Many patrons had been dining there since their youth.

A young entrepreneur and his wife acted quickly and made Silvia a lucrative offer. They would take over the eatery. The name would remain the same, and if allowed to borrow the recipes, she would receive royalty payments, in addition to the money from the sale of the restaurant. Silvia agreed and handed over the recipes... well most of them. She kept a few tucked away as a promise to her parents. She was no fool. Some things are simply not for sale no matter the price. The new owners not only kept the original restaurant open; they opened a chain across three states in the South. Although Silvia has no official ties to the place, she conducts interviews with cooking shows on behalf of the restaurant when requested. She also makes herself available for photoshoots, and other activities surrounding the business when requested. With the money she received from the sale, she invested some, sent her family a portion and she decided she'd live off the rest. She traveled the world, spoiling herself by splurging on many things that brought her joy. She soon settled back into home life and found it too boring. She missed cooking for the masses. When she heard the renowned Wilkes family of Memphis was hiring a part-time chef for a major event, she lent her expertise. They hit it off and the rest was history.

She catered many meals for their family gatherings, business luncheons, and public events, which included the likes of local and national celebrity guests from around the world. This included politicians and their wealthy friends, and those in the medical field. She was able to do what she loved, without the added stress of running a restaurant. When people realized that the Wilkes' had secured her as one of their chefs, they were a bit envious. Many tried to steal her away with lucrative offers, but she remained loyal to the Wilkes and Brockington family. Silvia wasn't a live-in employee, although she does have a private suite at the property. She enjoyed her time with the Wilkes family, and they were her number-one priority when she was on duty. She kept the household employees in line, which came easy for her due to her background in running her own restaurant. Her duties seemed to morph from that of a chef, into more of the house manager. She was in charge, and nothing was done concerning the household or its staff without her say. Her word was final, and it was respected even among her employers. Another perk of the position was, that she was able to spend time with her favorite guy friend, Samuel. Samuel enjoyed seeing her first thing in the morning when arriving at work, and he would express it by bringing her a single yellow rose each Monday. A moment she looked forward to.

Today was the day of his golf game with Peyton and Gil's fathers, and he was excited to spend some special time with his friends. Peyton's father is an attorney, and Gil's father is a primary care physician. The men often took some time away from their respective practices for their favorite game of golf. Mr. Samuel waited patiently for Gil to come down the stairs.

Peyton looked up from feeding the baby and asked,

"What time will you be home today?"

"Baby, it's going to be a late day. I'll call you when I get a break. With another quick peck, he said, "I love you,"

"Love you too."

Gil hurried down the floating marble staircase. Samuel, dressed in plaid slacks, a blazer, and golf shoes, stood at the foot of the stairs, waiting with Gil's things. He greeted his employer with a warm smile and then helped him put on his suit jacket. He gave him his briefcase, which had wheels.

"Are you sure you don't need me to drive you today Mr. Wilkes?"

"No sir Mr. Sam. I'll be a little late this evening, so I'll drive myself."

"As you wish. Have a fruitful day young man."

"You do the same, Mr. Sam. Oh, and have a great golf game. Tell Pop and Dad I'll see them this weekend. I'm gonna whip you old men and win my money back," he said smiling. The men would sometimes bet on their golf games using pennies. No real money was exchanged. It was all for sport. Samuel said, "Wishful thinking young man. By the way, you still owe me twenty cents.

"Put it on my tab Mr. Sam. You know I'm good for it. Anyway, you'll be losing it back to me come our next game."

"I don't think so, but stay encouraged, son. Perhaps you'll win one day soon, but I'm sure I'm going to win the next one," Samuel said, teasing him. After giving Samuel a friendly pat on the shoulder, Gil left for the clinic.

Gil Wilkes is an award-winning, board-certified plastic surgeon in Tennessee, with more high-profile clients than anyone in the South. He owns a four-story, state-of-the-art surgery center with the latest technology in the heart of the city. He also owns real estate around the globe including properties in the Memphis area, mainly luxury condos, which he rents to celebrities and the wealthy elites frequenting the state. He also uses one particular property for his high-profile clients after their surgeries.

Due to certain risks, he's not particularly fond of them flying immediately after surgery, and he recommends they stay close, in case any complications arise. The units are staffed with full-time, on-call nursing, full concierge services, and other amenities, allowing his clients to continue to recover in the comfort and luxury to which they're accustomed.

Gil has a team of highly skilled professionals at the top of their class in the medical field, opting to work with only the best. He also teams with surgeons in other states when they require his assistance. They trusted Gil because they knew their patients would be in capable hands. His attention to detail and his knowledge of the human anatomy makes for not only a flawless surgery resulting in amazing results for his clients but faster healing times. He takes pride in his work. He cares deeply for his clients. He lectures at top medical schools all over the country, and he continues his groundbreaking research on the human anatomy.

On this day, he had two surgeries; one was on the wife of one of his colleagues, and the other was on a male patient who wanted a nose job. He also had several consultation visits and will be checking in on his post-surgery clients. He went on to perform his surgeries which lasted a total of seven hours combined. Afterwards, he showered, grabbed his slacks, a shirt, and a tie from the closet, and quickly got dressed. He looked at the clock and noticed it was going on five-thirty. At his request, Silvia prepared Basmati rice, with chicken tikka masala for his lunch. He was eating later than usual. He put his food in the microwave. While his food was warming in the microwave, he called Peyton for a FaceTime chat. They chatted for a few minutes until the microwave beeped.

"Hey babe, I have to go. I'll be home in a few."

"Okay Honey, we'll see you soon, I love you," Peyton said.

"I love you too."

Gil pulled his food out and hurriedly ate his meal. After about thirty minutes, his receptionist informed him of the last client. He gulped down a few swallows of bottled water.

As he stood to his feet, ready to greet his client, two large Italian men dressed in designer suits stepped into his office. Gil was taken aback. He was sure his client was supposed to be a woman.

"Are you Dr. Wilkes?" one of the men asked Gil.

"Yes, I am," Gil answered, looking perplexed.

The other guy went over to Gil and patted him down for weapons. Gil stepped back in protest.

"Hey, what's going on here?"

"He's clean!" the man said.

"Clean? Are you guys with the police or what? If so, why are you in my office?"

The larger guy backed away from the office door. In stepped a tall, malnourished Italian lady. Her grey designer pantsuit hung loosely from her thin frame. She was wearing a large hat and dark sunglasses. She turned and faced the men who were standing guard at Gil's office door and said,

"Giovanni, Frankie, please give me some privacy."

The men stepped outside. Once they were gone, she stepped into his light. She lifted her head and looked at Gil. His heart dropped. Although her face was severely marred, he recognized her as Delilah Castellucci, wife of Dante Castellucci. Before she married into the Castellucci family, she was a Hollywood actress. Gil was all too familiar with her movies, as Peyton enjoyed her romantic comedies, forcing him to sit through many hours of what he called *"Chick Flicks"* on their date nights. Delilah made her mark in many blockbuster hits alongside famous male co-stars, and for a time, she enjoyed great success as major roles came her way. Her striking beauty, toned body, and lavishly long legs made her the envy of women all over America, especially those in the entertainment industry. She now stood in Gil's office, a shell of her former self.

One could only imagine why a woman of such beauty would allow a surgeon's scalpel to touch her face, let alone completely butcher it. Perhaps it was the pressure from those in the entertainment industry seeking more youthful actresses, as she was passed up for two major roles, which she so desperately wanted. She was no longer playing the darling girl next door or starlet with innocent aspirations of a bright future. Those roles were given to younger actresses, while she was asked to play the more mature roles. It was a sign that she was aging in Hollywood years. She wanted to keep a leg up on Mother Nature, so she had cosmetic surgery. Her life has changed since the surgery, a surgery that her husband Dante begged her not to have. Gil knew of Dante and the rumors of his ties to organized crime. He also knew he wanted nothing to do with this potential client.

"I'm Delilah Castellucci," she said, lifting a skeletal hand covered by a thin layer of pale skin. Gil was nervous. His hand trembled as he extended it to shake hers. Swallowing the lump in his throat, he said,

"I'm Dr. Wilkes."

"No need for introductions; I know exactly who you are," she said. "You're one of the best plastic surgeons in this state. I'm very familiar with your work. I saw what you were able to do with jazz singer Kitty Malone. You took twenty years off her appearance. Oh, and the talk show host, Lydia, looks amazing. It seems you're a well-kept secret in Hollywood until the tabloids caught Kitty leaving your clinic. Lydia openly admitted that you performed her surgery. Now, the entire entertainment industry is raving about you. Your work precedes you. I've seen the many miracles you've performed on some of the direst cases. I wish I'd heard about you much sooner. I've had some work done. But I'm not satisfied. I need you to reverse the damage that's been done. I want you to repair my face."

She removed her shades and hat. "Look at my face. I went in for a simple facelift, eyelid surgery, and nose job and this is the result." Gil had a ghastly expression on his face. Being a devout Christian, he rarely swears but he couldn't help but feel a few profane words rise inside, but he refused to let them roll off his tongue. Her face was severely disfigured. She had huge splotchy, red cheeks from bad injections; her lips were protruding from her face in a droopy fashion. With a crooked nose and lopsided brows, her eyes were set in a widened state. She hardly looked human but more of a macabre, cartoonish figure. The scarring around her scalp line and behind her ears was unbelievably visible with a keloid appearance. Due to the botched job, she suffered from severe depression and extreme weight loss. Her bones protruded through her skin. Gil leaned in for a closer look. He knew it would take extensive work and possibly three or more surgeries to attempt to repair the damages to her face and the scar tissue. It would be a high-risk surgery, and the results were probably not going to be to her liking.

"Mrs. Castellucci; whoever performed your surgery did you a disservice."

"There were two different surgeons," she said. "Dr. Thomas Burke was the one who performed the first few surgeries. Then Dr. Aaron Rhodes performed the follow-up surgeries. All totaled were six surgeries. Neither of them produced the results I was seeking. Needless to say, my husband wasn't pleased. My acting career is over. I rarely leave home. This has put a strain on my marriage. My husband can't stand to look at me. He doesn't take me out with him in public anymore. He rarely comes home and when he does, he sleeps in another room or pretends to be too busy to interact with me. He leaves me sitting in a large empty home with no one to talk to. I used to be the jewel in his crown, now he's disgusted with my appearance. I've visited many surgeons, and it seems as if no doctor is willing to help me."

Gil said, "I've never seen these many mistakes, even among new surgeons. Actually, it's the worst I've ever come across. It was almost as if they were deliberately trying to destroy your face. Are you sure they were board-certified?"

"Dr. Burke came highly recommended by fellow actress, so I went for it. What I didn't know at the time was, that she was sleeping with him, and the timing wasn't coincidental. Turns out we were both up for the same part in a huge production. After allowing him to perform the first surgery, I allowed him the option of trying to fix his mistakes. The results were bad, so I went to Dr. Rhodes to have him reverse the damages and the outcome was far worse than expected."

"Were these American surgeons or did you have the work done abroad?"

"Yes, I had the work done here."

"Did you verify their credentials? I can't readily say that I've even heard of either of those physicians before, and I know most surgeons in the industry. You must do extensive research before you go under the knife. One or both of your surgeons caused significant damage to your face and frankly, I'd feel uncomfortable performing any work on you. I wouldn't want to risk doing further damage or far worse, facial paralysis. I'm sorry but I can't do the surgery. You probably need to continue your search to see if there's anyone else who'd be willing to help you."

Gil said this in hopes that she would go away. Actually, he could perform the surgery and the outcome could prove beneficial, but since other surgeons had already botched the job, he didn't want to get involved. The other reason was his concern about rumors of her husband's ties to organized crime. After realizing who she was, he didn't want to have anything further to do with her. She was under the impression that he could reverse the damages and return her face to its natural appearance, but she would look vastly different, and he didn't want or need the trouble. His gut was telling him this was not someone with whom he wanted to do business.

She stepped back after hearing the news. She produced a slight frown then raised her distorted eyebrow and said,

"I'm sorry, but do you really think that I'll take no for an answer?"

"Ma'am you don't understand the risks."

"I understand that you've done this before. I happen to know you're the best. I've seen the before and after photos of other botched surgeries you've performed, so you can do this for me."

"Ma'am, those surgeries were not the same as yours. Another concern I have is I can see you appear to be severely malnourished. I'm not sure your body could even handle such an invasive surgery in your frail state. It's my professional opinion that you shouldn't have any surgeries at this time. You could be permanently scarred for life."

"I'm already scarred, so I'm willing to take the risk. Besides, I believe in you, and I know that if anyone can successfully perform this procedure, it's you. If it's a matter of money, I'll let you know I'm willing to reward you handsomely in the sum of your choosing. My influential and powerful husband will see to it that you will want for nothing. His influence reaches far beyond the financial realm. All you have to do is ask. Trust me; taking advantage of this opportunity would be in your best interest."

Gil stood firm on his decision. He didn't want to discuss the subject any further. He was exhausted and he was ready to go home to his wife and child. Slightly annoyed he said,

"Mrs. Castellucci, I can't in good conscience take on your case. I'm simply not the surgeon for you. Thank you for coming. Have a nice day."

He motioned for her to let herself out, and then he returned to his seat, expecting her to leave. Visibly disappointed, she exhaled. She proudly lifted her head while putting her shades and hat on and said,

"Thank you for your time, doctor." She stormed out. Giovanni, the head of her security team, could tell she was upset. After helping her inside the vehicle and now sitting in the driver's seat, he looked in the rearview mirror and asked, "Is everything alright, Mrs. C.?" Delilah, with her arms slightly crossed, pouted.

"Not at all, Giovanni?"

"Is there anything I can do to make it better? Perhaps, persuade him to cooperate?"

"I'd like that very much. My husband would want that. You know he'd want you to do whatever it takes to make me happy."

"I'm on it, ma'am. Just leave it to me and the boys." Delilah sat back in her seat. Giovanni exited the parking lot heading towards the airport. Frankie followed suit.

Although nervous, Gil knew he'd made the right decision. He sat at his desk and thought about the uncomfortable visit. The fact that she came in with armed guards who frisked him on his property and demanded that he operate on her angered him. She was bad news from the start. He was glad to be rid of her and her goons.

He brushed off the visit and began thinking of Peyton and his daughter, smiling. His day was done. He gathered his things and left his office, heading for home. He stopped by the florists and purchased a bouquet of flowers and a pink teddy bear for his daughter.

"Babe, I'm home," he said, rushing up the stairs to find Peyton."

"I'm in here babe," she said. He could tell she was in the nursery. He smiled and trotted towards the nursery. He went inside. Peyton was putting the baby down for a nap. She was wearing a very light sheer nightgown that opened in the front. Gil walked up behind her, placed his arms around her waist, and kissed her on the neck. She looked down and saw the flowers. She chuckled a bit as she took them from his hand.

"You look gorgeous. Oh, and you smell amazing. Is that a new perfume you're wearing?"

"I'm not wearing any perfume babe. I don't want to wear anything that may irritate the baby. It's just soap," she said. He embraced her and inhaled her scent. She turned to face him. She gave him a few pecks on the lips. "The flowers are lovely," she said.

"They're not more beautiful than you, my love." After flirting with his wife, he looked over in the baby's crib at his daughter. She was lying on her back in a peaceful sleep. He placed the teddy bear next to her and lightly caressed her cheek with his finger. "She has so many stuffed animals. It's beginning to look like a jungle in here," Peyton said, looking around at the other stuffed animals Gil had brought home.

"I'm sorry, I can't help it," he said. Seeing them made the stresses of the day disappear. He turned to Peyton again scanning her from head to toe. She was soft and sexy. Her breasts were engorged with milk. He lightly cupped them with both hands. "I see you're loaded," he said teasing her"

"Yes, she didn't have much of an appetite. I need to pump."

She walked towards their bedroom. On her way, Gil said, "Do you need help?"

"She chuckled, "I think I can manage"

"I want to help"

"I bet you do."

"She took out her breast pump. She sat on the bed and got comfortable. She pumped the milk with Gil's help. Well, he mostly watched in amazement. After she was done, she stored the milk for future use. She cleaned herself and she signaled to Gil that she wanted an intimate evening. They made love, and she slept soundly in his arms…….

The following morning, Peyton woke up to feed the baby. Gil had already left for the day. He didn't want to wake her. He knew she could use the sleep. There was a knock at the door. It was Clara, their nanny. Clara Nunez was a Mexican national, who had come to America on a work visa. She was working towards becoming a US citizen with help from the Wilkes'. Since Peyton was an attorney, she knew the ins and outs of helping immigrants become naturalized citizens and had already taken on several cases successfully. Peyton was in the process of helping her nanny so she, too, could become a citizen. Clara, now in her early forties, was never able to have children. She'd married when she was younger with the marriage only lasting a few years. After her failed marriage, she sought work in Mexico as a housekeeper for wealthy families. The work was long and grueling. With bratty children and elitist wives who belted out strict demands, many employees were abusive and treated her unfairly. Not to mention their horny husbands, with their constant, unwanted sexual advances towards her. She felt powerless and often gave in to the pressure of having sex with her employee's husbands out of fear of losing her job.

Most of her friends her age were living in America. They sent word of the money they were making and the many opportunities afforded them. Unmarried women who had no children were free to make the most money. One of her friends contacted her with the information needed, and she left for America. She made more money as a live-in nanny. In addition to her job, she worked to become an American citizen. She was paired with the Wilkes family, which she enjoyed. Working for them was a far cry from the horrid conditions in her home country, and she easily settled into her new job.

"Good morning, ma'am," she said in a thick Spanish accent. "I'm here to relieve you. Ms. Silvia is on her way up with your breakfast."

"Thank you, Clara," she said. Clara leaned over and lifted the baby from her mother's arms. She played and talked with the baby. After she left, Peyton's breakfast was delivered. After eating, she showered and went downstairs to check her emails. On her way, she saw Samuel. He was busy shining a few pairs of Gil's shoes while humming an old blues tune.

"Good morning, Mr. Sam," she said

"Good morning, Mrs. Wilkes," His eyes lit up when he saw her. The sun was brightly shining where he was seated, and one could almost see their reflection in his polished bald head. He was clean-shaven; his dark brown eyes donned crow's feet, and his eyebrows were greying. His unmistakable warm smile showed his perfectly straightened teeth. Teeth so perfect, that Peyton was curious as to whether they were dentures.

Although curious, she knew it would be inappropriate to ask. It didn't matter anyway. He was still quite a handsome man for his age. She also knew her chef, Silvia, admired him. They were the absolute perfect couple who thought they were keeping their relationship a secret, but everyone knew they were an item. They simply wanted to maintain a sense of professionalism on the job.

Peyton walked over and kissed him on the cheek.

"How'd the golf game go with you and Dad yesterday?"

"Oh, I let him win. You know how your ole daddy is. He can't take a beating."

She smiled and said, "Sure you did, Mr. Sam." He laughed and said, "Nah, child, he beat me honest this time. I'm just glad I didn't bet money on it. I would've lost at least fifty cents." After a little laughter, Peyton changed the subject.

"Are you coming to the christening?"

"Of course, I'm coming. I wouldn't miss the opportunity, which reminds me." He set aside the shoes and his polishing rag and walked into the foyer to retrieve several packages. Then he went back to where Peyton was standing. He handed her two large gift bags and an envelope.

"This is for the little princess."

Peyton looked inside the bag. She was amazed at the cutest gifts he had picked out: a brown baby doll, a pink and white lace dress, and matching shoes with Grace's initials embroidered on them.

"Oh, Mr. Sam, look at you. These are so cute," she said of the dress and shoes.

"I was hoping you'd like them. Ms. Silvia helped me pick them out. It took a few days to narrow down what I thought would be the perfect gift for the little angel."

"You're the best, Mr. Sam," she said, giving him a warm hug." She then opened the envelope and pulled out the contents. "US savings bonds; how thoughtful of you, Mr. Sam."

"Yeah, that's not all; look at the other one." She took a look at the rest of the documents in the envelope. "Our little Gracie now owns a few shares of MSP stock. It's been on the rise for some time now. It's a hot deal. I hear it's a good sound investment. It'll be worth a fortune once they go through with the merger."

"Oh, I'm speechless, Mr. Sam, but this is too much. The dress and the shoes were enough. We can't take this gift, although it's very generous of you."

"I won't take no for an answer."

"But Mr. Sam, can you even afford something like this?"

"Not only can I afford it, but my estate is also well planned, thanks to your father. I had a load of cash just lying dormant in the bank. With your father's wise advice and some fancy paperwork, my children and I are set for life. So, you see, my dear sweet child, you're looking at a wealthy man."

He let out a chuckle and winked. He then whispered, "Can I let you in on a little secret?"

"Sure, Mr. Sam."

"I'm not here for a weekly paycheck. I'm here because I love you guys. You're like family to me. I enjoy coming to work every day. It gets me out of the house and keeps me alive and vibrant. I enjoy my coworkers, especially Ms. Silvia; she's amazing. I get to golf with my friends and enjoy life. Being a part of this family helps me do just that, so money is no issue. I purchased these things for Grace and want her to have them. She's the closest I'll ever get to having a grandchild since my own children haven't given me any. I guess that's why I love volunteering at the elementary school so much. Hearing the children calling me Grandpa Banks makes my heart glad. So please, accept my gift for Grace," he said. With his head slightly tilted, he pleaded with her through eye contact and a convincing smile.

The last thing she wanted was to offend him. She was moved to hear him speak of them as family, and the feeling was mutual.

"Mr. Sam, please accept my apology. I'll gladly accept this very thoughtful gift on Grace's behalf. Thank you again," she said, hugging him one last time.

He helped her put the gifts away and went about his daily tasks. Peyton made her way to her computer and checked her emails. Afterward, she reviewed the files of her father's clients from the Brockington Law firm. She was still a part-time attorney. She had stopped practicing law for a short time, trying to pursue other goals, but when her dad became ill, the doctor advised the overworked attorney to rest to stave off more health issues. Peyton began filling in for him, especially on his high-profile cases. After scanning over some of the documents, she called her mother.

Peyton's mother is a clothing designer. She owns a boutique with one-of-a-kind designs and an online store where she sells her apparel. She contracts with several outside businesses that design jewelry and other accessories to incorporate into her work. It is a highly successful business.

"Morning Ma. Did I catch you busy?"

"Not really. I was just putting the finishing touches on Grace's christening gown. You ought to see it. It is so adorable. She's going to look so pretty, like a little angel."

"Send me a picture when you're done."

"No, it's a surprise; you'll have to wait until the day of the ceremony."

"Aww, Mom," she said in protest.

"Don't *aww mom* me. You'll see it soon enough."

"Okay, I guess I can wait. Where's Dad?"

"He's at the office. He has court later this morning."

"Okay; I must let him know I'm going to sit in on the deposition for the Atkins case. I'll highlight what's needed for the arguing points for a better settlement."

"There you go again, still trying to work. You need to think about the baby. Don't be worried about your father and his clients."

"Mom, since the heart attack scare, I promised I would do all I could to help him."

"Yes, and you guys won that case. Your father promised that he would allow the other perfectly capable attorneys he'd hired to handle any upcoming cases when it was over. You need to rest. Enjoy time with your baby. The years go by so fast. It'll be over before you know it. You'll look up one day, and she'll be in high school, then college. Then she'll bring home a husband of her own just like you did. You'll miss all of it from working so much. I enjoyed my life of raising you and supporting my husband, and now I get to enjoy spoiling a wonderful grandchild. I have no regrets. Make sure you can say the same."

Peyton knew her mother was right, as always. She would take her advice, and although she enjoyed motherhood, she still wanted to help her father at the law firm. She minimized her hours while doing most of her work from home.

"I'm heeding your advice, Mom," she said, reassuring her. They chatted briefly before Peyton ended the call to prepare her father's case.

CHAPTER TWO

It was the day of Grace's christening ceremony. Peyton was hurrying to gather everything she needed. This was a special day, and it had to be perfect. She wasn't taking any chances. Gil was positioning the baby's car seat while Clara was caring for the baby. Gil had returned inside, noticing Peyton sprinting down the steps in heels.

"Baby, why didn't you take the elevator? Rushing down the stairs like that in heels, you're going to hurt yourself. You need to slow down. It's okay to be a little late. The church isn't going anywhere. They'll wait for us. Besides, we're not late. Service doesn't start for an hour and a half."

"I know, but I'd rather be there too early than too late. It never fails; whenever we try to be on time, something pops up to make us late."

"Well, don't kill yourself running down the stairs, or we'll be headed to the emergency room instead. Next time, take the elevator."

"Okay Honey. Stop your fussing. Let's go."

Gil took the baby's bag from her shoulder and carried it to the vehicle. He helped his wife inside. Clara placed the baby in the car seat and locked her in. She then buckled her own seat belt, and they headed to the chapel. When they pulled onto the property, Peyton noticed her father's car was already in his assigned parking space. They had already gone inside. Since Peyton's mother held a position on the church board, she went into her office to drop off a few items she would need later.

It was forty-five minutes until service time. Peyton took the baby to the nursery, where she used that time to bottle-feed and change the baby's diaper. Clara was on standby in case her assistance was needed. Peyton's mother made her way to the nursery as well. She was dressed in a light cream-colored dress with a very elegant hat. Her clutch was firmly gripped under her arm, and the christening gown and other accessories were in a large gift bag. She placed her clutch on a nearby table and walked over to the rocking chair where her daughter was seated. She kissed the baby's cheek. "How's Nana's little angel?" She said, talking baby talk to Grace. "Are you ready for your big day?"

"I know I'm ready to see that gown you've been keeping a secret," said Peyton. Peyton motioned for Clara to finish feeding the baby. Her mother handed her the box. Peyton was anxious to see how the gown looked. When she opened the box, her jaw dropped.

"Mom, this is so lovely. This is by far one of the most magnificent garments you've ever created. She ran her fingers across the silk white Duchesses fabric. She admired the crystal beadings and the pearl beads along the neckline and front of the gown. She was floored when she saw the lace overlay. Silk ribbons were donning the garment, and a matching bonnet. Peyton teared up.

"Oh, Mom, I'm going to ruin my make-up," she said. Mrs. Brockington took out a tissue from one of the nursery's stands. Peyton blotted the tears that formed under her eyes.

"Thank you, Mom. Now I see why you refused to send me a photo. I love it."

"Nothing's too good for my granddaughter. Thank you for allowing me to make it. It was truly an honor."

"We wouldn't have had it any other way, Mom," she said.

Gil's parents arrived. Mr. Wilkes sat on the second pew, taking a seat with Peyton's father. Mr. Brockington informed Gil's mother that the women were in the nursery. Mrs. Wilkes joined the others in the nursery. After the baby was dressed in her gown, the ladies gushed over how beautiful she looked. She had large, light brown eyes like her mother. Her light brown hair was silky and curly. She had the cutest dimples, which appeared as she laughed uncontrollably while the women played with her. They went into the sanctuary. Peyton was surprised at the many guests. They took their places. Gil looked at his wife, who wore a lovely, elegant, pristine white gown. Her diamond earrings sparkled as she looked down at the baby. Her hair was pulled back with a diamond-crusted comb. She looked refreshed and beautiful. He was a proud husband and father. At that moment, he knew his life was truly complete. He was grateful to God for all that he'd done in their lives, and he thanked him under his breath. Pastor Hawkins stood before the podium. "Will the grandparents of this beautiful child please come forward?" The Wilkes' and Brockingtons stood with their children. The pastor began the ceremony by reading a few scriptures, and then he said,

"Jesus said, *"Let the little children come unto me, for such is the kingdom of God."* Saints, please join us in welcoming our newest and youngest member, Miss Grace Marie Wilkes, daughter of Dr. Gilbert and Peyton Wilkes."

Pastor Hawkins prayed and dedicated her to the Lord. Afterwards, they all mingled in the banquet hall, where the guests presented their gifts to the family. Peyton and Gil were seated in separate chairs. Gil held his daughter while Peyton greeted the guests. Each guest brought their gift and blessed the baby.

"Hello, Mrs. Wilkes. I brought this for the little one. She's so beautiful." Peyton looked up to see who was handing her the gift and to thank her. The lady wore a glamorous blue pastel pantsuit. She wore a silk scarf on her neck and a large pastel hat on her head. Peyton noticed she was wearing a large pair of sunglasses. Gil was focusing on the baby and making sure she was okay. After briefly looking at the woman, he swallowed the lump in his throat. His heart was beating rapidly. He gripped his daughter, holding her close to his chest. The woman was none other than Delilah Castellucci. Peyton didn't recognize the former actress. What little of her she could see was marred, so she chose not to stare. She shook her hand with a warm *"Thank you,"* Delilah stepped aside. While Peyton was speaking to the next guest, Delilah looked over the top of her shades with an evil glare aimed at Gil; she narrowed her eyes and then lifted her shades back on the bridge of her crooked nose. She produced a half-hearted grin and slowly walked out with her two goons by her side. She didn't make a scene; her presence was enough of a statement. Gil placed the baby in Peyton's arms. He hurried outside to confront her. He noticed her black SUV pulling away from the church parking lot. He was livid. She'd manage to turn a sacred event into a hellish moment. He'd killed once before to protect his family, and he knew if forced to do so, he'd kill again. He immediately thought he was no match for this gang of criminals.

He didn't tell Peyton of his concerns or about the initial visit. He was, however, planning on informing the police. Gil wanted to separate Delilah's gift from the others. He wanted nothing to do with her, but by the time he returned, Clara had already packed it away. They continued receiving visitors as Samuel and Clara placed the gifts in the car that Samuel drove to store them. There were so many of them that they thought they would need a moving van to transport them back to their home. Once the vehicle was packed and ready, Gil went to the family vehicle, personally placed Grace in the car seat, and then drove his family home. He continued glancing in the rear-view mirror the entire way to ensure they weren't being followed.

Once he got his family home safe, he went into his study to see if he could find any information on the Castellucci family. He pulled up several news stories on the search engine. There were the many accomplishments of Dante Castellucci; pages after pages touted his latest business ventures. He was praised for his philanthropic works. Although there were many rumors and speculations online of Castellucci's having been involved in many murders and violent crimes, they resulted in no arrests. Not only that, but his attorneys had also filed several lawsuits against anyone who publicly slandered or defamed his name and character by accusing him of crimes without proof.

By all accounts, he seemed like a great guy, and the people loved him. He'd managed to charm the public and they couldn't seem to get enough of him. Gil looked up Dr. Burke, the plastic surgeon who performed Delilah's initial surgery and found disturbing news. He was killed in a fiery car crash soon after her surgeries. The other surgeon, Dr. Rhodes, died in a fire in his home. There it was in black and white; both surgeons who'd botched Delilah's surgeries had mysteriously died, and their violent deaths were considered accidents.

Neither incident pointed to Dante Castellucci, but Gil felt in his gut that he was responsible. Now, his wife was on his doorstep, asking him to perform an already difficult surgery that had possibly gotten two other surgeons killed. He knew if anything happened to him and his family, they would indeed make it appear accidental, and none would be the wiser. It appeared as though the Castellucci's were allowed to freely roam the earth and harass the citizens at will.

He leaned forward in his chair. With hands to his temples, he stared at the computer screen. Feelings of frustration and anger flooded his being. Something had to be done if he wanted to get a handle on this situation. His first plan of action was to beef up security at his home. He called Hal, the head of his security team.

Hal retired early from the Memphis police department and now works for the Wilkes family. He was a large husky white male; six foot two, head shaved bald. He was a former wrestler in his younger days. He continues to dabble in the sport in his spare time. His position was primarily laid back. He supervised six security officers at the Wilkes' estate. Two of them worked for the Memphis police department and now work part-time for the family. The other four were retired military and professional security guards. There were never any real threats to the home; they were just warding off any potential threat by their mere presence. They manned the security booth for home deliveries and guests of the couple.

It had been a week since Delilah Castellucci's visit. Gil was still a bit uneasy, so he remained on high alert. It was a Saturday evening, and Peyton had yet to open the many gifts she'd received from the baby's ceremony. Since it had been a week, she wanted to send thank you notes to everyone. She called her mother over so they could go through the gifts together. She planned on keeping some, especially those personalized for the baby. She planned to donate the rest to the church for the needy.

Another one of their employees, Jan, was on hand to throw away the boxes. Clara was seated with them. She held the baby as they looked through the packages. After about an hour of admiring the many gifts, Peyton happened upon the box that Delilah had given her. It was a mid-size box, wrapped with yellow gift wrapping and a lime green bow. There was an envelope stuck on the back of the package. She read the envelope. It read, *"To your beautiful baby girl. Keep an eye on your family."* It was signed with the initials D.C. Peyton was puzzled by the message.

"Who is that from?" her mother asked.

Peyton handed her the card.

"It has the initials D.C."

"Do you remember who gave it to you?"

"No, I can't remember. There were so many guests; I can hardly tell you who was there. Between Dad and his friends, Gil's associates, and our church family, there's no way to tell who gave us this. There were possibly a couple of hundred people in attendance."

"Well, open it and see what's inside."

Peyton shook the box a little and heard glass rattling inside. "Sounds like it's broken, whatever it is." She opened it carefully. Inside was a small porcelain doll. The face had been shattered. Affixed across the chest of the doll was a surgeon's scalpel.

Peyton threw the box with its contents on the floor. Her mother gasped,

"That's one strange gift."

"It's creepy, no doubt," said Jan. In a panicked voice, Peyton yelled, "Gil!"

Gil was in his study. The way his name was called indicated that it was urgent, so he came running.

"What is it, babe?" She signaled for him to look at the doll with its shattered pieces on the floor. He saw the small box lying at her feet. He bent over to pick it up.

"What is this?" Peyton frantically handed him the card.

"This card was attached to the box."

Gil immediately knew what the message meant. He was absolutely sure of the sender when he saw Delilah's initials. This was now a direct threat to his family. Confident that he could handle things safely, he still didn't tell his wife. He didn't want to alarm her. He did, however, tell her that he'd beefed up security and was placing several more guards outside. She didn't make a fuss; she let him have his way.

It was nine-thirty a.m. Monday morning. Peyton had showered and fed the baby. She allowed Clara to take her while she finished her work. She was sitting at the breakfast nook with her laptop. Gil ran downstairs, fixing his tie as he went.

"Hey babe, have you seen Mr. Sam? He was supposed to bring my suits and my shoes. I can't seem to find anything. He hasn't called to let me know whether the car is ready. I don't want to be late."

"Honey, I don't think he came in today. I didn't see him when I went into the kitchen. I thought you had given him the day off because he's normally here by six o'clock."

"No baby, and if he's running late by chance, he'd call me so I can make other plans."

"Well, check with Ms. Silvia to see if she's heard from him. If anybody would know of his whereabouts, it would be Ms. Silvia. They're practically joined at the hip."

Gil checked with Silvia, who was cleaning the stove. "Ms. Silvia, have you seen Mr. Sam?"

"I haven't seen or heard from him this morning. I was hoping to see him. He hasn't called, but he's on the schedule to work. When I saw him yesterday at church, he told me he would be here. He missed bringing me my special rose, and I didn't receive my morning phone call. Perhaps he got a little busy. It's still kind of early. He may be here soon." She continued cleaning.

After checking with everyone else in the home, he only got more of the same. He hadn't called anyone, and nobody had seen him. Gil thought it was strange, but he continued his morning without his favorite helper. After calling Hal at the guard house to have his car brought to him, he kissed his wife and went to work. He performed the first two scheduled surgeries that day. Afterwards, he went to check his messages. His receptionist interrupted him on his way to his office. "Dr. Wilkes. I didn't want to bother you during surgery, but you received several urgent phone calls from Mr. Samuel Banks. He says he needs you to return his call right away." Gil, who was concerned he was sick, promptly returned his call.

Samuel Banks- "I could never forget a face. Especially not this one. I recognize this young man. I met him at the coffee shop. He's an enormous guy. With his towering height and boulder-sized head leading to a broad neck, he resembled a prized fighting bull. His very appearance is quite intimidating. That's why he stood out among everyone at the shop. I haven't seen many Italian men in this area, and I've lived in Memphis all my life. He held the door open for me a few times. I'm now aware, that it was no coincidence that this guy would be at my coffee shop, at the same time as me for three days in a row. Yeah, I should've seen this coming. But how could I know he was up to no good. He made me believe he was having car trouble. Little did I know that helping him would lead me to my current predicament. I thought he was a kind young man, but judging by the way he's been beating me, I know that's not true. My ribs are sore. I don't know how much more I can take. Lenny is his name. At least, that's how everyone else in the house addresses him. They're all Italian men, each one more intimidating than the next. The largest of them all is some chap named Frankie. His stoned shoulders, bulging muscles, and massive fists feel like a Mack truck hitting me. He has a short fuse and is very abusive. He doesn't seem like he wants to be here. He acts like this job is beneath him. I try not to look at him too much. It seems to anger him. The ringleader appears to be a mysterious-looking woman. She looks oddly familiar. It's like I've seen her somewhere before, but I can't quite put my finger on it. She wears strange clothing. Turtlenecks, scarves, and shades indoors. They're calling her Mrs. C. She's belting out violent demands. She speaks mostly English. Every other word seems to be in Italian. I hear her speaking of possibly harming my friends. I know they're planning on killing me even though they say they're not. They have to. I've seen their faces. Why would they keep me alive? Numbness has set in on my hands, which are zip-tied and resting on my lap. My feet are loosely tied. I can move them, but not by much. Trying to escape is futile. I'd fall flat on my face. Besides, this house has too many rooms, and I can't tell which way is out. I'm on the second floor. From where I'm seated, I can see power lines, the tips of trees, and the rooftops of the other homes in the area. My body's sore. My jaw is weighted with swelling. Gasping for air, I'm suffocating due to a possible broken rib cage. I'm in and out of consciousness. When I come to myself and realize I'm not in control. I feel helpless. The imminent threat is unnerving. Perhaps they would be doing me a favor if they ended my life. I can only hope Mr. Wilkes doesn't give in to her demands. These people seem to know everything about us. She mentioned my coworkers and my boss's family, including little Grace; all of whom I deeply care for.

Grace is the closest I'll ever get to having a grandchild. My darling Silvia will never know how much I truly love her. I didn't want to press her. I never thought I'd love another woman outside of my dear Gloria. Silvia is a great woman...Sigh... I suppose I should've told her that I'd fallen for her. Now it's too late to make her my wife—no sense in wallowing in regret. Thoughts of my children Eli, Pam, and Sam Jr. are causing feelings of remorse. Their many offers for me to visit more often went unanswered. I should've visited more. Father my prayer to you is, when this ordeal is over, Mr. and Mrs. Wilkes and my children are safe, and these evil people brought to justice. I want my children to know I love them. My last prayer is that the beatings stop. I don't think I can take another blow. Just take me now so this suffering can end."

As Samuel prayed and contemplated his life, Delilah snaked her way up the stairs. She walked over to the seating area where Samuel was sitting. He was in a recliner in the corner of the room. She's carrying his ringing cell phone.

"Answer the phone. It's the doctor," Delilah said. She pressed the call button and then placed the phone up to Samuel's face. Samuel answered. There was static on the line.

"Mr. Wilkes!" he said with a muffled voice through his swollen jaw.

"Mr. Sam, we got a bad connection. I can barely hear you," Gil said. "Can you speak up a little?"

Lenny said in a deep, baritone voice, "Your butler, Sam, is tied up right now, and he can't take your call. But he wants to leave you this message." Gil heard a loud, blood-curdling scream coming from Samuel. The man got back on the phone and said,

"Follow our instructions; he won't be harmed; if not, the consequences could prove deadly. If you involve the police, he won't be the only one who'll need reconstructive surgery."

Gil was alarmed. He knew this was nothing more than Delilah Castellucci resorting to violence to get her way.

"What do you want from me?"

"Someone will be in touch soon with instructions."

"So that you know, he's not my butler; he's family. There are a lot of people who love him, including me. He's a good person. Please, for the sake of his family, don't harm him."

"No harm will come to him or your little family if you do what you're told."

When the man mentioned his family, his heart sank. He immediately thought of Peyton and Grace.

"Please, mister, leave my family out of this."

"If you're concerned about their safety, just comply with our demands. You'll hear from us within the next twenty-four hours."

The call ended abruptly. Gil felt like he was going to pass out. He began to hyperventilate. He slowly stood to his feet. He frantically paced back and forth. A burst of angry energy overtook him. With a closed fist, he slammed his hand against the wall. A sharp pain went through his hand up to his wrist. He knew he'd injured himself but, at the moment, he felt no pain, only anxiety. He shook it off. He immediately called Peyton, but she didn't answer. He called the house phone, but Jan, Silvia nor Hal answered. Neither did anyone at the guard house. He thought about involving the police, but he remembered what the guy on the phone said. He hurried home to check on his family. When he got there, he noticed the guard house was unmanned. He couldn't find Hal. He was alarmed. He felt he was walking into a trap. He feared for Peyton and the baby but had to check on his family. He cautiously went on through the gate. He drove down the winding driveway and up to the house. He ran through the large house frantically looking for his wife.

"Peyton!" he yelled in a panic.

"Peyton!" He couldn't find her. He hurried up the stairs to their bedroom. He retrieved his handgun from the safe and continued looking for his family. He looked inside the nursery. After running back down the stairs, he noticed Peyton coming inside wearing her apron and gardening gloves. She was carrying a basket that contained some freshly picked vegetables. She'd been working in her garden. He hid the gun in his waistband so she couldn't see it.

"Baby, where have you been? I've been calling you?" he said out of breath. "I was working in the vegetable garden. While I was gathering lettuce, I found a family of rabbits. There were so many that I needed help. We called the wildlife office to have them come out and relocate them. We need someone to come out and place barriers up, so they can't get in the yard. They practically destroyed all the lettuce. I managed to save these."

"Where were Hal and the other officers? I called the guardhouse, but neither of them answered the phone."

"Well, I asked them for assistance. Everyone was outside dealing with the bunny debacle."

Out of breath, Gil stood with his hands on his hips. Peyton passed by him, looking him up and down. She noticed his hand was red and swollen.

"What happened to your hand?" she asked, placing her basket on a counter. She reached for his hand. He had been running on adrenalin, so he hadn't noticed the swelling.

"Oh, it's nothing," he said briefly, looking at his hand... "I had an accident at the office. Where's the baby?"

"She's with Clara. She took her for a walk out on the property."

"Call her and tell her to bring my baby now. You know what, better yet, call her and I'll send Hal for her as well."

Peyton looked at Gil puzzled by the aggressive tone in his voice.

"Gil, what's happening with you? You haven't been yourself lately; it seems like you've been on edge. Is everything okay with you?"

Still not wanting to alarm her, he said, "I'm okay baby. I just have a lot on my mind. Seriously, I need you to call Clara and have her bring Grace inside."

"Okay, I'll call her now."

While Peyton called the nanny, Gil called Hal. After Clara was safely inside with the baby, he called a meeting with Hal. He was reluctant to tell him about Samuel, but he knew he had to tell someone, so he decided to trust him. Hal had driven the golf cart down to the house. Gil got in and sat on the passenger side. Hal drove them away for privacy. "Hal, I have a serious problem."

"What is it, Mr. Wilkes?"

"Hal, what I'm about to tell you is confidential. I need you to promise me that you won't utter a word of what I'm about to tell you. It's a matter of life and death. Do you understand?"

"I understand, sir."

"Mr. Sam has been kidnapped. The person holding him has threatened to harm him if I don't meet their demands."

Hal lifted his shades onto his bald head to make eye contact with his employer. "Someone has kidnapped old man Sam?"

"Yes, and not only are they threatening Mr. Sam, but they're threatening my family as well. I didn't want to go to the police because I didn't think it was that serious, but now they have Mr. Sam. I'm afraid they're going to harm him."

"Mr. Wilkes, You must inform the police. Although I'm no longer a police officer, I'm still required to report a crime once it's been made known to me. I'll have to report this to the police.

They're capable of handling this. You need to trust them. We may not see Mr. Sam alive again, but by not saying anything, you're almost guaranteeing his death. Even if they move forward with their threats, by reporting this crime, we can give the police a head start. They can then at least protect your family."

"Hal, please don't do anything yet. Give me twenty-four hours. Let me see what they want. Then, after that, you can call the police. I mean, they're not going to kill him unless I refuse to comply with their demands. Perhaps I can get clues as to where they're keeping him. If we go to the police now, we'll lose all hope of getting him back alive. He means too much to us. I have to at least try to get him home safely. I can't lose him, Hal; I just can't. I'm begging you, don't say a word."

"Well, can you at least tell me who you think has taken him?"

Gil was careful not to tell Hal, especially since he had already shown interest in reporting the kidnapping. He couldn't risk him tipping off the Castellucci family. He kept the information to himself."

"Hal, I'm not quite sure who has him. I just received a call that he was being held. I was allowed to speak with him for a brief moment. He was alive when I last spoke with him. That's all I can tell you. When I learn something more, I'll let you know."

Hal rubbed his chin while looking downward. He wasn't convinced that keeping quiet was the best option. He wasn't in agreement with what Gil was requesting of him. He almost hated that his employer had placed him in this difficult position. He, too, had grown fond of Samuel over the years. Samuel touched the lives of everyone he met. Everybody loved him. He was thoughtful and caring. He was wise beyond belief. He was the last of a dying breed. Hal was heartbroken at the news and desperately wanted to help Samuel. Against his better judgment, he decided to go along with Gil's plan, at least for now.

"Sir, I'm going to give you twenty-four hours, then I'm going to call the authorities. It's never wise to deal with kidnappers alone. The department has trained personnel who specialize in such matters. You going it alone will most likely get the old man killed. You really need to rethink this."

"I've thought about it. They want something from me, so there's no way they will harm him unless I don't meet their demands. I'm going to hear them out. Getting the police involved at this point would be a bad move. We'll probably never see him alive again. I'm not willing to take that chance."

Hal drove Gil back to the house. Although he was concerned, he would wait until Gil gave him the go-ahead before reporting the kidnapping. Hal met with the rest of his security team and warned them to be on high alert for immediate threats.

CHAPTER THREE

Gil and Hal gathered the Wilkes' staff together. Without mentioning Samuel's kidnapping, they were told of the real possibility of a threat. Gil felt it best to allow the employees time off until the immediate threat was over. No one wanted to leave. Each member of the staff was adamant that they stay on board. They didn't know how serious the situation really was. Silvia, who was among the staff members, was also gathered in the room. She thought it unusual that she hadn't heard from Samuel. She noticed that he had not come to work that day and wasn't at the meeting either. She felt in her gut that something was wrong. She looked toward Gil and Hal and asked, "Where is Sam?"

"Mr. Sam is going to be okay, Ms. Silvia," Gil said, trying to remain calm. Silvia noticed the gloomy expression on Gil's face. He's normally a friendly, calm, upbeat guy. She'd seen the look before. When he and Peyton separated, Gil began to lose hope, thinking they would never reconcile. Silvia would try and comfort him during that time. Now she noticed the look again. It was one of worry and hopelessness. She knew he was hiding something. She addressed him.

"I called Sam all morning, and he hasn't responded. He normally stops and gets a newspaper, coffee, and my yellow rose, but this morning he never showed. I couldn't reach him by phone, so I called the elementary school, and they informed me that he didn't show up for story time either. So again, where is Sam? You said he will be okay; that means you know something."

Gil noticed Silvia's anxious expression. It was apparent that she was concerned about his well-being. Gil looked towards Hal. He could tell Hal wanted them to know the truth for the sake of all involved.

"Okay, Ms. Silvia, Mr. Sam has been taken. Someone wants a favor from me. If I give them what they want, they've promised to return him unharmed. Hal and I will be working with the Memphis police department. We will do everything within our power to get Mr. Sam home immediately. We don't want any of you to become targets of these people; that's why we want to give you some time off until we can resolve this."

Silvia responded, "I'm not going anywhere. I'm staying right here. I want to be here when he comes back." The rest of the staff expressed love and concern for Samuel. They all opted to stay. Hal said, 'I want you to understand that the threat is real. You could become a target by choosing to stay in this home. Nobody will fault you for wanting to leave."

Jan, Silvia, Clara, and the guards all chose to stay with the family. They were informed of the safety precautions they needed to take from that day forward. Clara was briefed on the safety of the baby. The guards were not to leave their posts under any circumstances.

Although Gil had yet to tell his wife about the kidnapping, his paranoid behavior set off alarms with Peyton.

Peyton was seated out back, enjoying the beauty of the man-made lake. She watched as the geese flew overhead with loud honking while gliding in to make their landing. As they settled into the lake, resting from their long flight, she enjoyed the sunset, which cast a beautiful portrait in the southern sky. A great blue heron strutted across the water's edge, plopping his head in the lake for a nice meal of frogs or fish. He was indiscriminate. He would eat anything at the moment. Peyton was sipping her favorite cup of hibiscus tea with a hint of pomegranate juice. She was lost in the scenic views. The serene atmosphere was comforting. Who needs a television with views this breathtaking? God's display played out wonderfully during all seasons of the year. The sights, sounds, and smells of nature were an otherworldly experience. This was her desired place to be out of the grand palace-styled mansion, luxurious interior designs, and expensive art collection. A place where she would meditate often, gather her thoughts, and relax. Gil had a feeling she was out there, and he was right. He trotted towards where she was seated. She was startled when he suddenly appeared and said,

"Babe, I don't think it's a good idea for you to be out here right now."

"Gil, you scared me. You made me spill my drink on my blouse. It'll probably be ruined," she said while blotting at the crimson liquid with her napkin.

"I'm sorry, baby. I didn't mean to frighten you. Let's go inside," Gil said, looking around the perimeter of the grand yard.

"Please tell me what's going on."

"I'm sorry, I can't right now."

"So, there is something wrong, isn't there?"

"Look, Sweetheart, it's best not to involve you. The less you know, the safer you'll be."

"What do you mean by safer? Are we in danger?"

"It's nothing, really," he said, trying to downplay the situation. "Let's just go inside for now." As they were moving towards the house, Peyton asked,

"Does this have anything to do with that strange package we received by courier today?"

Alarmed, Gil stopped briefly and said, "What package?"

After making it inside, Peyton got the bubble-wrapped envelope and handed it to him. He opened the already-opened package. He saw a money clip. He recognized it as the one he'd given to Samuel.

Gil decided to tell Peyton the truth. They both were seated on the chaise.

"Peyton, I need to tell you something important."

"What is it, honey?"

"Listen, our family is in danger?"

"I knew you were hiding something; what's going on?"

"Last week, someone with whom we're familiar came by my office."

"Well, who was it?"

"Dante Castellucci's wife Delilah.

"Are you talking about the actress?"

"Yes"

"I always wondered what happened to her. She just seemed to drop off the face of the earth."

"Yeah, well, she's popped up on my doorstep, and I'm unhappy about it."

"Honey, I'm confused. Why would her visitation put us in danger?"

"Delilah wants me to perform surgery on her."

"Babe, she's just another A-list celebrity coming to you for surgery. You should be excited to add another one of Hollywood's elites to your clientele. So, what's the problem?"

"The problem is she needs an extensive amount of work done. She's under the impression that I can perform a simple surgery and make all her problems go away."

"Well, you're one of the best; why should this surgery be any different from any of the other difficult surgeries? You *are* the surgeon most clients come to when all others fail. Why didn't you take this job?"

"Because any surgery performed on her won't make her appearance better but will further damage her already disfigured face and baby, she looks bad; I mean really bad. She looks nothing like she does in her movies. She's unrecognizable. She thinks I can make her look as she did before she had all the work done, and that's not going to happen. I informed her that I wouldn't do the surgery."

"Again, how does that put us in danger?"

"Her husband, Dante Castellucci, is rumored to have ties to organized crime. Delilah and her henchmen came to my office, bullying me around. Now, she's been threatening me with her creepy presence. She was at Grace's dedication ceremony. "You know that creepy doll with the shattered face, scalpel, and the note?"

"Yeah,"

"Well, that was her doing. And there's one more thing you should know. The reason Mr. Sam hasn't shown up for work is because she's kidnapped him. He was allowed to speak with me by phone. While talking with him, I heard him screaming in the background. I think they may be torturing him."

Peyton gripped his arm. "Oh no, Gil, she has Mr. Sam?"

"Yes, and they told me not to go to the police, or they'll kill him. I told Hal so he could properly protect us. I want to notify Mr. Sam's children. I'm torn. They have a right to know what's going on with their father. I'm afraid that if I tell them, they'll go to the police, and it may be dangerous for Mr. Sam. They say if I perform the surgery, they'll deliver him safely, and no harm will come to my family. They seem to already know so much about us. I must tell you, I'm afraid this won't end well. I googled the two surgeons who botched Delilah's surgeries and baby; get this: both were killed in suspicious fires. I know this surgery isn't going to have the outcome she's expecting, and when the results aren't pleasing, I'm afraid she'll take it out on us. I don't think I can keep us safe as long as we're on their radar. That's why I've added a step to ensure our safety until this is over." Peyton thought of her parents.

"What about Mom and Dad? Are they safe? What about your parents and our daughter? Oh, Gil, I'm afraid!" She was in a state of panic and began to cry. Gil took her by the hand and tried calming her, all the while trying to put on a brave face.

"Listen, baby, I understand your fears, but I have things under control. Our parents are going to be okay. I've hired an independent security team. They are the best of the best. The government contracts with them when foreign leaders or federal witnesses need protection. These guys are military-trained in special weapons, combat, and protective life-saving skills. They'll protect us and our family for now. Delilah mentioned to me that her husband's influence goes a long way. We don't know who the enemy is. Dante Castellucci could have someone on the police force. You know how these things work. That's why I hired this new security firm. They were expensive, but they're worth it. I'm willing to pay any price to keep my family safe. They will be arriving around noon tomorrow. That's the earliest they can be here. Hal will be here to protect you guys until they arrive. In the meantime, I'm going to have to perform the surgery."

Suddenly, the phone rang—dead silence. He and Peyton looked at each other. Gil looked over his shoulder at the phone. He was hesitant to answer it. He stood to his feet and slowly made his way over to the phone. It suddenly stopped ringing when he was about to pick it up. Hal's voice came over the intercom.

"Mr. Wilkes, there's an urgent call for you."

Gil hurried and answered the phone.

"This is Gil."

"Have you had a change of heart? If so, I'm ready to work with you."

Peyton looked on nervously, wringing her hands. She could tell by the look on her husband's face he was speaking with Samuel's captors. It was indeed Delilah.

"Yes, ma'am, I have reconsidered my position on the matter."

"I'll be in town tomorrow at eight a.m.," she said.

"Okay? But can you tell me whether or not Mr. Sam is okay?"

"He's okay for now."

"Well, can you let me speak to him so I can know for myself?"

"Hold the phone please," Gil anxiously waited. It took a few seconds.

"Hello"

"Mr. Sam, are you alright?"

"I'm alright Mr. Wilkes; Just ready to come home." Samuel sounded drained like all the life had been sucked out of him. Peyton moved closer to Gil. He placed the phone on speaker so she could hear. She desperately wanted to say something to Samuel, but she knew whoever was holding him would be listening, and she didn't want to be on their radar. She remained quiet and sobbed.

"Just hold on Mr. Sam. Everything's going to be alright. We're going to get you home real soon, okay."

"I wish that were true young man, but I don't know if they will let me leave this place."

"Don't lose hope, Mr. Sam. Remember, we love you." Delilah's voice could be heard on the phone.

"As you can see, your butler is alright. Now I'm looking forward to seeing you in the morning. Don't try anything stupid, Dr. Wilkes." She abruptly ended the call. Hal had been recording the call for the authorities.

Gil put the phone back on the charger. Peyton fell into his arms and cried out loud, "Gil, please; do whatever you have to do to get him back."

"I will babe." They comforted each other. Given Delilah's actions, he knew she was dead serious. He wasn't sure if she was a killer herself or if she simply allowed her husband's cronies to do her dirty work. Either way, he wanted to remain positive so he could get her out of his life as soon as possible.

Gil got word from his security team that both of their parents were okay, and their homes and businesses were being monitored. Neither Gil nor Peyton got much sleep that night. Gil's hand was throbbing. He could tell by the swelling that he had either broken bones or bone contusions. He soaked it in ice. Instead of allowing the baby to sleep in her nursery, she was placed between Gil and Peyton, who protected her through the night.

Hal wanted to escort Gil to his office, but Gil was dead set against it. It was risky for Gil to go alone, but he couldn't risk Samuel's life. He'd do anything to get Samuel home safe, even if it meant putting himself in harm's way. He was also aware that he was being watched, so he traveled alone. Without regard to his own life, he proceeded to his clinic. When he arrived, he noticed a couple of black SUVs partially blocking his parking lot's entrance. The building is a three-story structure, a mini hospital of sorts. There were many other offices inside, which Gil leased to dentists, primary care physicians, and several other businesses. The building had a small cafeteria and a gift shop. Frankie, a passenger with whom Gil had already met, stepped down from the SUV and motioned for Gil to open the door on the passenger side. Gil popped the lock, and the man got inside. He scanned Gil for potential bugging devices, asking him, "Are you wired?"

"No," Gil responded. "And I haven't notified the police either. In case you're wondering." After Gil was checked, the man motioned for him to continue driving.

Normally, Gil would park in the designated employee parking lot, where a magnetic key card was needed to gain access. Filled with rage, he pulled his car into the nearest parking spot and then purposely slammed his brakes. Frankie, who wasn't wearing a seatbelt, was thrust forward. His head hit the windshield, cracking the window. Bloop.... Gil heard Frankie's head when it hit the glass and his neck when it popped. He felt a small sense of gratification, although he knew he'd created a potentially dangerous situation for himself. He smiled inside. An embarrassed Frankie tried to remain cool as his head began to throb. He massaged the back of his neck to ease the pain. Furious, he looked at Gil and said, "Alright, Doc. Don't get cute. Try something like that again, and I'll kill you on the spot. You're lucky my boss needs you, or I'd make you pay for that." He rubbed his forehead. He could tell a knot would form.

The Castellucci crew had taken over his building and there was little he could do at the moment. Although angered, he fully cooperated. He complied with their demands. The other armed goon, Giovanni, met him at his vehicle. As he exited, he was thoroughly searched for weapons and forced inside. As he entered the building, Gil noticed that everyone was going about their business as usual. Some even greeted him. The Castellucci clan focused their attention solely on Gil's immediate office and his employees. They didn't involve others outside of the Wilkes Surgery Center. His personal staff was now a part of the events and pained him. Although his employees and colleagues weren't aware of the events taking place, they were taken aback by the presence of guards escorting the woman. They were used to seeing celebrity clients with at least one guard, but this client had guards that stood out from the norm. Rumors began to swirl as people wondered who she could be. When Gil went into his office, Delilah was already seated. This was his very own personal space. It was a space specially designed by his wife. There was a living area as well as a sleeping area. The décor was very posh. It resembled a nice condo-style suite and hardly an office, only because of the desk and seating area. Even that area was glammed up by Peyton's design team. This place was an addition to his home. He and Peyton spent many nights there before they had baby Grace. They often wondered if she was conceived in this very office. It was filled with memories. It was all he could do to keep from letting her know what he thought of her and her goons, who were invading this space.

Delilah was sitting her *unwanted ass* in a seat that his wife picked out. With one long, thin leg crossed over the other, she had a confident but smug expression on her face. An *"I told you not to screw with me"* smirk. Gil was seething. She invited him to have a seat in his own space. He went behind his desk and then slowly sank into his seat. Frankie and Giovanni stood to either side of him. The other two goons were standing in the doorway of his office.

Delilah uncrossed her legs and stood to her feet. She wore an all-black pantsuit. She removed her large hat and shades and placed them on the seat beside her. She slowly inched towards Gil's desk. She placed both of her hands on the desk, leaned forward, and said,

"No need to be angry. If you cooperate and all goes well, we'll be in and out before you know it. No one in this building knows anything. They'll remain safe if you don't inform them of what's happening. We see no need to involve them; however, they've been asked to cooperate fully. They believe this situation is a high-ranking official operating on a national security basis. While they're not being held at gunpoint, don't think for one minute that my guys won't hesitate to put a bullet in one of them if they get in our way. We came well prepared. We have plenty of backup.

And besides, this building could be loaded with explosives, which could kill everyone within a three-block radius." Gil's mind immediately went to the news stories online of the fiery deaths of her last two surgeons. This statement from Delilah confirmed his suspicions that they were behind the fires. There were no explosives in Gil's building. It was merely a fear tactic. She stood straight and said, "Now, doctor, I'm ready for a more thorough consultation." Gil pursed his lips. He stood to his feet and said,

"We'll need to go to an examination room."

"Show me the way," she said, motioning with her hand. On the way, she grabbed her hat and shades, putting them back on so nobody could see her face. Giovanni and Frankie followed them. Giovanni motioned for the other two guards to leave the office and head back to the home where Samuel was being held. A driver stood watch in the parking lot, waiting to take Delilah back to her plane. There was a total of five henchmen who escorted Delilah to the clinic that day.

Delilah and her men followed Gil into the exam room. On the way, Giovanni looked at Frankie's forehead and said,

"Hey, you might wanna let the doc take a look at that lump on your head."

"Screw you, Giovanni," he said under his breath.

"Hey, where'd you get that from anyway?"

"I don't wanna talk about it."

"Oh shit! Doc gave that to you, didn't he?"

"Just shut up and keep walking," Frankie said, feeling the knot and seeing how big it had become. Delilah and Gil went inside while the men stood guard at the open door. She eased her slim frame down in the exam chair. She removed her hat, scarf, and sunglasses. Gil began to look at the damages. He then had his nurse take several photos of her: first, a front view, then from both side angles. He then showed her the damages that needed repair and explained the difficulty of doing so in more detail. He took his marker and outlined the areas of most concern.

He then asked her a series of questions about her medical history, lifestyle habits, and extracurricular activities. She was a heavy smoker and drinker. She indulged in a little cocaine, and she was also on anti-depressants and other pills. She was exactly the type of client that doctors fear. She was extremely malnourished and the most unlikely candidate for the invasive surgery that she was seeking. Her current state of health would make any surgeon's job difficult. She had about a twenty-percent chance of a positive result, and that would be if she'd stop the drug and alcohol use, the anti-depressants, and at least gain a few pounds. He tried explaining the facts to her, but she was adamant about having the surgery that day.

It was final. He was given no other choice than to give in to her demands. He mentioned his injured hand to buy some time so that Delilah could sober up enough for surgery. That way, he'd avoid an interaction with the anesthesia medication. He mentioned it to her.

"Mrs. Castellucci, as you can see, I have an injured hand. It will at least need to heal."

She realized that she had overlooked his hand. She noticed it was red and swollen. "I'm going to need full use of my extremities to perform the extensive surgeries that you're going to need, and trust me, you're going to need at least three surgeries over several months."

She felt dejected. She'd received the same counsel from almost every surgeon she sought. It didn't matter how much money she had or how many threats she'd given; killing Gil or any member of his family or staff wasn't going to change the fact. Her face was damaged, and it would probably never be repaired. Here's a great surgeon with an injured hand, and any hope of help she could've gained by having Gil perform the surgery quickly faded.

A tear fell from her cheek as regret began taking over. Gil noticed. He rolled his stool back to reach for a tissue on the counter. Giovanni grabbed him by the shoulders to ensure her protection.

"It's okay, Giovanni," she said. Why don't you two step outside for a minute? If I need you, I'll call you."

They did as they were told. Once they were out of the room, she leaned forward. She reached her hand out to touch Gil as he was still sitting on the stool.

"Dr. Wilkes. Please accept my apology for the trouble I've caused you and your family. Most surgeons have given me the same prognosis. I just thought that things would be different since you were one of the top surgeons in the field."

"Mrs. Castellucci, I took an oath to do no harm. I care about my patients. They're not just customers to me. Once I perform their procedures, I feel that, in some way, we're connected. We develop lasting friendships here. I would never perform work on anyone if I knew I couldn't better their situation. I want you to be pleased with your results. Also, my clients are walking billboards. My name and reputation are on the line. Your appearance looks vastly different from your acting days. Yours is a worst-case scenario. If I'm unable to repair these damages, I'll be blamed for the outcome. I've worked hard in this industry to develop a great reputation. I've written books, and with my vast research on the human body, my articles have been published in medical journals and studied by my colleagues. I've been asked to speak at some of the top medical schools in America and abroad. Trust me; I know what I'm doing. If your damages can be reversed, I will tell you. I can perform the surgery, but it won't produce the results you're seeking. I'm not even sure you can survive the surgeries needed in your frail state. What you're insisting is that I participate in your death. If you insist on moving forward, you may not survive."

She exhaled. She began to sob. Gil felt awkward as she leaned on him for comfort. Bile rose in his gut as feelings of anger began to flow through him. His family was under siege. Samuel was being held against his will, and he was feeling helpless. Now, he must comfort someone he feels belongs in jail and he wants to be the one to put her there. Perhaps if he pretended to care, she would have a change of heart and release Samuel. He placed his arm around her shoulder to comfort her. He tightened his grip as he remembered Samuel's cries for help. Gil was conflicted because, on the one hand, he thought choking her out would be a perfect punishment; he had never hit a woman. He was against it. He was tempted.

He held his composure and continued to comfort her.

"Dr. Wilkes. I feel I have no other choice but to move forward. I'd rather die trying than live not knowing what could've been. You don't know what feeling trapped in this body with this face is like. Children are afraid of me. People stare in horror. My own mother pauses when she sees me. I used to be so beautiful. People loved me. They loved looking at me. There are photos of me everywhere. I was known for my beauty, but now I look like this…this horrid thing, a beastly creature of sorts. I can't go on this way. I've already decided that if this doesn't work, I'm taking my own life. I refuse to go on looking like this. You're my only hope, a last-ditch effort to save my marriage and my life. I'm asking you to proceed with the surgery regardless of the risks."

"Alright," Gil said with a stern warning in his voice. "It's your call. Should I give you time to call your husband or family to make arrangements if you don't survive?"

She didn't answer him. He looked her directly in her soulless eyes as she stared into nothingness. She seemed to be caught in between this world and the next.

"Mrs. Castellucci," he said a little louder to bring her back from her temporary trance.

"I'll be okay," she said. She could see the stress on Gil's face. Knowing his butler was missing, she feared he wouldn't be up to his best performance. With that and the hand injury, she said, "In the event that I don't make it, my husband will know what to do. I can't promise he won't take things out on you or your family, but I can at least make a phone call before the procedure to safely return your butler."

Gil exhaled. The flood of relief that flowed over him quickly faded with the realization his family was still in danger due to a slim chance of her surviving the surgery. A surgery he'd be performing with an injured hand. That, coupled with the thought of explosives being involved, he was back at square one. Gil helped her up from the exam chair. He called for his staff. He had his nurse prepare a steroid shot for his hand. While the nurse was injecting his hand with the medicine, Delilah stepped away and made a phone call to her men who were holding Samuel. Lenny answered. "Lenny, we're going into surgery now. How's our visitor doing?"

"Well, Mrs. C., we've got a problem."

"What do you mean? Has he escaped?"

"No, it's not that."

"Well, what's going on?"

"You see, one of the boys got a little too rough. I think the old man is dead."

The news angered Delilah. Although she'd made death threats to the family, she hadn't actually planned on anyone getting seriously hurt. She hadn't counted on the depths that her guys would go to in order to get the job done. She was no killer. She didn't know if her husband was one. She enjoyed his reputation of being tied to organized crime because she usually benefitted from the rumors alone. She was also aware that after she'd make complaints to her husband, certain people would either be killed, *accidentally, of course*, went missing, or indicted on some trumped-up charge. She didn't have proof her husband was behind the carnage, but she had her suspicions. Dante made a point about not involving his wife in his personal business. Only he and his crew were privy to the ugly side of the business.

Delilah began scolding Lenny.

"I told you I wanted him alive. Now, we've lost all bargaining power. I didn't think we would have to go to plan B. It's too risky. They are sure to involve the police if we do."

"He's still alive, Mrs. C., but barely. He took a pretty good blow to the head. He started mouthing off. You know the boys don't like it when they mouth off. He was being disrespectful, so they had to teach him a lesson. He ain't gonna make it, so the boys are going to get rid of him."

"Dump him Lenny, and go to plan B."

"Okay, plan B it is."

"And Lenny, someone's going to answer for this."

She ended her call. She didn't mention the incident to Gil. She was taken away and prepped for surgery.

CHAPTER FOUR

Peyton was home nervously awaiting word from Gil. She wanted to go out by the lake and pray but was too frightened. She was in her large, posh bedroom, pacing back and forth with her baby girl in her arms. She refused to allow the child to leave her side. She was too stressed to breastfeed, and the baby was becoming fussy. Clara came inside to help her. Sensing her mistress was stressed; she brought Peyton some warm tea to calm her.

"Mrs. Wilkes, I brought you some chamomile tea. Please have a seat and allow me to care for the baby. Peyton was reluctant to let go of her baby. When she realized she was being a bit dramatic, she allowed Clara to take the baby. That way, she could sip the hot tea without the risk of burning her baby. After all, Clara was sitting within arm's reach. Peyton took her tea and eased down on the bedroom sofa. Clara had also brought a warm bottle of breastmilk for the baby. She sat in a lounger across from Peyton and fed baby Grace. Peyton was babbling on, trying to get her mind off of the kidnapping. Sipping her drink, Peyton said,

"Clara, I don't know what I would do if it weren't for you. You've been so good to our family. You're an amazing caregiver. Gracie adores you." Having Clara there eased her anxiety. She was awaiting the surgery results or any word of when Samuel would be home. It was all she could do to keep from going to the police herself, but she did as Gil told her and remained quiet for the safety of all involved.

"Clara hummed a soothing lullaby in the baby's ear….Crash!!! Clara looked up when she heard the sound of glass shattering. The teacup that Peyton was drinking from hit the floor. Peyton had fallen asleep. With baby Grace still in her arms, Clara walked over to check on her mistress. She appeared to be unconscious. "Mrs. Wilkes," she said, calling Peyton's name in a low whisper. She got no response. Seeing that Peyton was passed out, she scurried to the nursery and gathered a few of the baby's belongings that were in an already prepared bag. She grabbed the light pink cashmere blanket that was in the rocking recliner and tightly wrapped the baby in it. She rushed down the back stairway and hurried outside into the garage. She jumped into Peyton's vehicle. She didn't bother to put the baby in her car seat. She placed the baby on the front floorboard and covered her, then went to the guard gate. She was met at the gate by the guards, who quickly waved her through. Neither of the guards noticed it was Clara, who was driving Peyton's car, except for one who had been compromised by Delilah, unbeknownst to the Wilkes.

Meanwhile, back at the clinic, Gil was getting prepped to go to work on Delilah, who had already been put to sleep. Ignoring the pain in his hand, he immediately began the surgery. He began at the scalp and painstakingly began working his way around the severe scarring. The task was long and grueling. She began losing blood. Her blood pressure was rapidly dropping. Gil worked feverishly to complete the surgery and minimize more blood loss.

The nurse was calling out the vital stats to Gil. The anesthesiologist was becoming concerned. After stabilizing her, Gil finished the last stitch. The surgery lasted a little over six hours. Delilah was wheeled into the recovery room, where she was closely monitored by Gil and two nurses. He was concerned for his family and Samuel. He wanted to call Peyton, but Giovanni and Frankie stood guard, waiting for Delilah to awaken. Although her blood pressure was low, she appeared to be recovering just fine. After about an hour, she finally came around. She was groggy. Gil stood at her bedside.

"Mrs. Castellucci, how are you feeling?"

"Was the surgery a success?" she mumbled.

"The surgery went well."

"What about scarring?"

"Mrs. Castellucci, I think you will be pleased with your results. It's not as bad as before. I worked hard to minimize any possible damages. You should be fine. However, I recommend two more surgeries for the best possible results."

"Do you have a mirror?" she asked groggily.

"Your wounds are wrapped for your protection. Your results will be better if you allow them to heal properly." She was insisting on seeing the results. Gil was forced to remove the gauze that was wrapped around her head and chin area. He motioned for one of the nurses to get them a mirror. While she was doing that, Gil lifted her bed so she could see. The mirror was placed in Gil's hand. He nervously handed it to Delilah. She looked at her reflection. Her face was beet red. Her appearance, although vastly different, was smoother and tighter. She took note of the stitching on her eyelids, around her ears, and her neck area. Her nose had a covering over it. She didn't recognize the face staring back at her in the mirror, but she could tell she was going to be okay. It was apparent that she would still be unrecognizable, and she was almost fine with that. She didn't want to have the stares, gasps, and negative attention from the public. Everyone in the room awaited her response. She didn't say a word. She slowly lowered her hand with the mirror down to her side. Gil took the mirror from her hand before it could hit the floor.

She was on an IV to help replenish her fluids and introduce much-needed vitamins into her body. She was offered a small of pain meds. Gil was desperate to learn about Samuel. He knew it probably wasn't a good time to ask, but he needed to know. Once Lenny informed Delilah about Samuel, she had Gil's baby held as added insurance until after surgery. Gil continued to monitor Delilah. He was physically and emotionally drained. He relieved his nurses to take their much-needed break. After they left the room, he looked at Delilah. He wanted so badly to be rid of her. He wanted Samuel home and his life back to normal.

In the meantime, Clara was at the meeting spot to drop off the baby to Delilah's men. She was in a secluded part of the city. A van pulled behind the vehicle she was driving. After flashing his headlights, the driver pulled alongside her vehicle. A passenger hopped out of the van. Clara had the driver's door open so she could retrieve the child and hand her over, collect her pay, and then leave. "Get in the van," the man demanded.

"Excuse me?"

"I said, get in the van." She did as she was told. Clara was forced to abandon Peyton's car, and they proceeded to another location. Before arriving, her cell phone was taken and destroyed. They finally made it to a large, luxury, two-story home. It was the last house on the street. The nearest neighbors were at least a block away. The owners were part of an online rental program and rented the home when they were out of town. The home was surrounded by a lush landscape, and a wall of trees separated it from the other homes in the area. There was a large three-car garage that was attached to the home, making it easy to carry a kidnapped victim inside unnoticed. The driver lightly tapped on the entry door. Lenny opened it. Clara was escorted inside by both men. Lenny took his weapon from his holster and motioned for her to come further into the room. They were near the kitchen area of the home. Once inside, Lenny said, "We don't have anybody to look after the kid. You have to do it."

"That wasn't a part of the deal," she said.

"That's not my problem."

"What about my money?"

"You'll get your money when we tell you, you'll get it. Now get your ass over there and take care of the kid."

When Clara realized that she was being held captive, she felt betrayed. She was promised that by bringing the baby, she would get paid and could leave town. Now she stood in a room with several dangerous criminals, and judging by their appearance, she had a feeling she wouldn't make it out alive. She was almost sure of it. Especially after overhearing them tell of how they'd dumped the body of the old man speaking of Samuel. She sank in her seat staring at the baby. Feelings of guilt, and regret flooded her soul. She teared up thinking of her betrayal. She wanted to escape but she knew it wasn't possible. She was stuck. Her fate was sealed, and she deserved every bit of karma she was about to face.

A few hours had passed, and Peyton was still asleep. She was awakened by Silvia, who had brought her dinner earlier. She was coming to claim the dishes so she could finish her cleaning for the evening. She noticed that she hadn't eaten, so she asked, "Mrs. Wilkes, would you like me to bring you something else to eat? I noticed you haven't touched your dinner."

Peyton lifted her head and tried to focus her eyes on Silvia. She made out her plump figure and the colors of her uniform, but her vision was fuzzy. She lay back down.

"Mrs. Wilkes, Are you okay?" Peyton began mumbling, trying to speak, but her words were inaudible. Silvia gently shook her. "Mrs. Wilkes!" Peyton slowly opened her eyes and shifted them upwards towards Silvia, who was directly in her face. She sat on the bed next to Peyton and lightly tapped her cheek. Peyton's eyes rolled back in her head, and she went limp in Silvia's arms. She gently placed a pillow under her head. After taking the dinner napkin from her food tray, she dipped it in the untouched glass of water and proceeded to wash Peyton's face. After a few minutes, she began to come around. Silvia was making a fuss over her. After the birth of the baby, Peyton had been keeping a hectic schedule. Silvia watched as Peyton seemed to bounce back faster than normal. She began to scold her.

"You young mothers don't know how to get the rest you need. You've been moving nonstop ever since that baby was born. I told you to slow down. You're going to have a setback. You've been working, taking care of the baby, and doing everything but resting. It's no wonder you're passed out up here." After about ten minutes of caring for her, Peyton began to wake from her seemingly comatose state. She looked up at Silvia and asked,

"What happened?"

"Your body is tired. That's what happened."

"Where am I?"

"You're home, in your bedroom, child."

"Where's my husband?"

"He hasn't come home yet." Feeling nauseated, Peyton tried to gather enough strength to sit up on her own. The sedatives that were in the tea that Clara had given her were enough to sedate two adult males. Peyton's memory slowly returned as she became aware of her surroundings. "Clara!" she yelled out in a panic. "Where's Clara?"

"Nobody's seen her or the baby for hours. I think she left." Peyton panicked. "Please Ms. Silvia, call the guardhouse!" She did as she was told and then she held the phone to Peyton's ear.

"This is Mrs. Wilkes. Have you seen Clara?"

"No ma'am. I saw your car leaving out of the gate a few hours ago. We thought it was you."

"I'm still in the house, as you can see."

"When we noticed your car leaving, we automatically assumed you were driving it, ma'am?"

"I need you to notify the police. Clara and my baby are missing."

Peyton called Clara's phone and got no answer. She ran into the nursery, hoping she would see her baby in the crib, but when she noticed it was empty, her knees buckled, and she slowly fell to the floor. "Gracie!" Peyton screamed. Silvia tried helping her to the nearby rocking chair, but she just lay on the floor clutching her daughter's blanket. After a thorough search of the property, it was clear that Clara had left with the baby. The guards watched the security cameras. They noticed Clara acting suspiciously inside the vehicle. Her head was wrapped in a scarf, and she had the baby in tow. She was allowed to leave without confrontation. Panicking, Peyton called Gil. He was allowed to take the call.

"Gil, where's Gracie? Did you authorize Clara to leave with our child?"

"No, I didn't. Where is she?"

"I don't know, Gil, I don't know," she said, sobbing hysterically. Clara gave me a cup of tea. Afterwards, I went unconscious, and when I awoke, Clara and Grace were gone."

Gil looked towards the men who were standing guard. "Do you have my daughter?"

"Relax, Doc. She'll be fine. We're holding her and the nanny for added insurance."

"You had Mr. Sam. I was told he would be released."

"And he *was* released."

"So why did you take my child?" Gil asked, fuming with hot rage. With a wolfish grin, Giovanni shrugged his shoulders. "Sorry, buddy; orders from Mrs. C."

Gil lunged toward the men. Frankie pulled his large fist back and slammed it into Gil's gut. The powerful blow knocked him to the floor. "That's for what you did earlier. Try something else, and I'll kill you for sure."

Peyton could hear what was happening in the background. She lost all hope. She whispered to Silvia, "Gra…..Gracie's been abducted by Delilah Castellucci." She fainted. Silvia called the police and told them of the baby's abduction and asked for paramedics. After making the 911 call, she notified the guards on duty by pressing the alarm. Peyton was taken to the hospital with a police car in tow for added protection.

Although Clara was the nanny, she had not been permitted to leave with the child, so she was named the abductor.

An eager young news reporter named Kali Thompson was listening to the police scanner. She decided to chase down the story. She was the first reporter on the scene. She realized it was the Wilkes' estate when she arrived at the address. She knew this was going to be a huge story. One of Memphis's own well-known and prominent figures was in trouble, and she wanted to be the first to cover the story. The Wilkes and the Brockington family were the elite of Memphis. They were known philanthropists and were loved by everyone in the state of Tennessee. The mayor was known to throw many galas in their honor to celebrate their many works throughout the community. They rubbed elbows with local and national politicians. Gil was also known as a celebrity surgeon and the son of Dr. Albert Wilkes, his father, who owned several family practice clinics in Tennessee and Arkansas.

Kali Thompson stood outside, respectfully awaiting the officer's return to their vehicles. As more police presence began to dominate the street, Kali was able to get an officer to speak with her off the record. Hello, Sir; I'm Kali Thompson with Channel Seven News. Can you tell me more about what's going on?"

"I can't say much about the case until I speak with my superiors, but I can tell you that we're looking for a female African American infant by the name of Grace Wilkes, who was last seen with her nanny, Clara Nunez. We're interested in the safe return of the abducted child. A missing child alert has been posted. That's all I can say at the moment. An official statement will be made to the media soon." Upon pressing him for further details, he gave a description of the vehicle and other basic information.

Kali remained on standby. After contacting her boss, she was permitted to work on the story, so they sent a camera crew to her location. Until then, she went on her social media page assigned to her by the station and went on a live newsfeed.

"Hello, this is Kali Thompson coming to you live from the home of Gilbert and Peyton Wilkes. We have learned that there's a missing child alert for the baby and her Nanny, Clara Nunez. Clara is a Hispanic female, age forty-three years old. She was last seen around four p.m. with the child. She's reportedly driving a white 2024 Mercedes GLE. License plates are vanity plates *Wilkes 02*. If you spot this vehicle or Clara Nunez, please call 911 or the Memphis police department immediately. Please stay tuned to Channel Seven for more information as this case continues."

Since Peyton was at the hospital, Silvia acted as a family liaison. She found recent photos of both Clara and the baby and gave them to the police. The police officer inquired about Gil's whereabouts. Unaware that he and his staff were being held captive, Silvia informed police that he was at the clinic performing surgery. The police issued an official missing child alert and a *B.O.L.O.* for Peyton's car. The car was immediately found through its built-in navigational system. It had been abandoned. The police processed the vehicle for clues.

In the meantime, Gil was being held captive against his will. Once the news story broke, Lenny called Giovanni and informed him that the police were looking for the baby. Lenny thought it would be a simple job, and they would be in and out of Memphis as soon as the surgery was over. Since Gil was a famous doctor and a beloved citizen, Lenny knew the feds would be on to them and feared they would get caught. As loyal as he was to Dante Castellucci, he didn't want to go to prison for him or anyone else.

Giovanni was just as concerned as Lenny, but he realized that he was in too deep. He couldn't do much, because Delilah was still asleep. He called Frankie into the room, and they tried to devise a plan on what to do next. No staff members were allowed to leave until the guys could sort things out. Gil's head nurse, Brenda, was one of the two nurses Gil had relieved earlier. She happened to check her phone for messages. When she opened her phone, the story of Gil and Peyton's missing baby was on the front of her news page. She began to share it with the other staff members. She wondered if Gil knew. Things began to feel strange. Although she didn't see any immediate threats towards anyone at the clinic, she did notice the look of concern on Gil's face. She began putting clues together. Something didn't sit well with her. All the guards appeared to be Italian. The partially hidden client, whose name wasn't given, was an Italian woman. She thought there was no way they could be government agents, but if they were, she was sure that Gil's missing daughter and this mysterious client were somehow connected.

She texted her family and friends and told them she was being detained at the clinic, and nobody was allowed to leave. When her husband got her text, he called the police department demanding to know why his wife was being held. The investigation began.

CHAPTER FIVE

Lethargic and barely awake, Delilah listened as Giovanni informed her of what had taken place. With his mouth close to her ear, he said, Mrs. C., the police are looking for the kid. I'm afraid we're going to have to leave immediately. It's only a matter of time before the police arrive."

"Help me, Giovanni. Get me out of here now."

Giovanni took her by the right arm and placed it around his shoulder, then lifted her from the bed. She whispered,

"Where's Lenny with the baby?"

"They're still at the holding spot."

"Tell them to meet us at the airport and bring the baby. My husband's plane will take us back to New York."

"What about them?" he said, looking at the staff. You know we can't let any of them go free."

"Get rid of everybody here and take the kid to the plane. We'll figure out what to do from there," she replied.

Giovanni informed Frankie of the plan. They gathered the employees together. Hearing police sirens approaching, the driver outside radioed Frankie to alert them that the authorities were close. Frankie panicked. "Shit, the cops! Giovanni, what're we going to do?"

"Calm down and stand guard. We can use these guys as leverage."

"Fuck that, I'm leaving! You can deal with this shit on your own. Besides, the boss doesn't even know we're here. He refused to help Mrs. C., and now we're stuck doing her dirty work. I'm not going to jail for her. You can stay if you want, but I'm leaving."

Frankie left. Giovanni called for the driver, who was stationed outside, and demanded zip ties. Criminals almost always had them handy. Giovanni gathered Gil and his staff and marched them to Gil's private office. "Give me your keys!" Giovanni demanded of Gil. Keeping his eye on the weapon pointed at him, Gil retrieved his keys from his desk and tossed them to Giovanni. Delilah's driver had come inside with the zip-ties and tied each of their hands behind their backs. Giovanni decided not to kill Gil or his staff because he didn't have a suppressor on his weapon. Firing it would cause a panic in the building. He took Gil and his staff members and forced them into a large closet where he kept his clothing, golf clubs, and other accessories, then locked them inside. Gil was devastated. After locking the office door, Giovanni went for Delilah as the other guy returned to the vehicle. "Hey Giovanni, we'll get caught if we don't leave now. I'm going to give you a few more seconds and then I'm leaving. Come to the side entrance by the street."

Giovanni went back into the recovery room to help Delilah. With an IV and monitors attached, he didn't know which, if any, she needed. As he lifted her from the gurney, the wires and tubing became entangled. Giovanni desperately tried helping Delilah. He felt pressured as the man on the radio informed him that he was leaving without them. With the realization of the inevitable, there were only two ways out of the clinic; one was going to prison, and the other was his freedom, so he chose his freedom. Since Delilah was too weak to walk on her own, he dropped her back on the gurney. Both men left, abandoning her to her fate. They arrived at the airport before the police could discover who they were and what they'd done.

Lenny, who had already boarded the jet, set a frightened Clara in the back of the plane with Grace in her arms. Giovanni and Frankie followed suit. Two guys were left behind to drive the SUVs out of town. They were long gone when the police arrived, and the investigation began.

Peyton was barely holding herself together. Her parents were by her side, and so was a female officer. She was inconsolable. She tried calling Gil. She told her parents and the police the truth about Delilah and the kidnapping of Samuel. Meanwhile, at the clinic, the first squad car arrived. They didn't notice anyone inside the clinic. With the knowledge that they were dealing with dangerous kidnappers, the swat team was called in as a precautionary measure. Also, hostage negotiators were on standby. The police made a phone call inside the clinic but got no answer. The building was surrounded by law enforcement. The task force proceeded with caution and began entering the building. They carefully cleared each floor, sorted out each worker, and released them into the custody of awaiting officers. They were held for questioning.

They noticed the offices in Gil's clinic were empty. Abandoned coffee cups were on the desks, but no one was in sight. They went room to room and found no one. On a hunch, the officer decided to double back and check again to cover his bases.

The men proceeded with caution towards Gil's office and flipped on the lights. Hearing muffled sounds coming from the back of the office, they investigated further. With a few forceful kicks to the door jamb, the door opened. Seven desperate workers were begging to be freed. The officers immediately began cutting them loose.

Once Gil was freed, he sprinted towards the recovery room, looking for Delilah. Much to his surprise, she was lying on the gurney where Giovanni left her. She was in grave condition, and she seemed to worsen after Giovanni accidentally pulled her IV from her arm and disconnected her monitors. "Wake up, you witch! Where the hell is my child?" He violently shook her, pulling her up from the bed. Her head flopped forward and dangled like a rag doll. She couldn't answer him. As he continued, an officer came inside and saw what was happening. He immediately pulled Gill away from Delilah. "Take your hands off of me. She needs to tell me where my child is."

"Calm down, sir. I can't let you do this."

"She's kidnapped my child, and I need to know where she's taken her!"

"Sir, this woman is unconscious and in need of medical attention. She's of no use to you. She needs a doctor."

"I am a doctor. I need to know where my child is."

"We're working on that now, sir. Please, step this way."

While Gil was speaking, another officer escorted him out of the building. First responders whisked Delilah away. Gil was questioned but was mostly combative and desperate to know his baby's whereabouts.

When the dust settled, Gil was reunited with Peyton, who was at the hospital, and together they comforted each other as they anxiously awaited news of their baby. Peyton's body violently trembled, and her heart fainted after getting the news that the police still couldn't find her child.

She was given sedatives to calm her. Gil underwent a health exam to ensure he was okay. His hand was x-rayed, and it was revealed he suffered no broken bones. He was given a brace for his injury. His hand was the least of his concerns. After a few hours of being in the hospital, Peyton was released into the care of her husband. They were given police protection and were escorted to their home. They could hardly recognize their home when they arrived at their entrance gate. It resembled a police precinct. Law enforcement set up a make-shift headquarters from their home. No one was allowed in or out without proper authorization.

Helicopters swarmed the city, and one hovered over the Wilkes' estate. Gil and Peyton's parents and other close family members were given full around-the-clock police protection. As a safety precaution, the feds took over the guard house and released all the Wilke's guards, including Hal. They were questioned for hours as authorities tried to get to the bottom of the whys and hows of them allowing Clara to leave the property with the baby unchecked. They felt the entire kidnapping reeked of an inside job that may have gone farther than just Clara's involvement.

The special security team Gil hired arrived at the home, but it was too late, and the police sent them away. All household employees and guards were questioned extensively. They were forced to leave the home until police could sort out friend or foe incidentally; they, too, were given protection since Samuel had been abducted. The only employee allowed to stay at their request was Silvia. She was eliminated as a suspect immediately. Anyone close to the Wilkes was given a full investigation. Everyone was transparent with the police and cooperated to the fullest. Eager to help, all employees willingly submitted to searches of their properties and electronic devices. The Tennessee State Bureau of Investigation, Memphis PD, The FBI, and law enforcement agencies from New Jersey were on the case. There was to be no stone left unturned.

The lead FBI agent, Brian Donavan, was in the home. Agent Donavon, a six-foot-two African American male, has been with the bureau for twenty-eight years and has been instrumental in bringing home countless kidnapped victims. He and his family were victims of a kidnapping when his oldest son was taken while on a trip to Mexico. The kidnapping was a direct result of Agent Donavon's work on a case that involved the arrest of several Mexican drug cartel members. After law enforcement's successful rescue efforts to bring his son home safely, the experience left him with greater compassion for victims who are suffering the same fate as his own family. Armed with that, and his thirty-plus years in law enforcement, he's known as a master negotiator and great agent. He introduced himself to Gil and Peyton as officers escorted them in and lead Detective Larry Sheppard, from the Memphis PD Major Crimes division. After introducing himself to the agent, he said, "Agent Donavan; we have the Wilkes family here. They're the parents of the missing child. I've spoken with them briefly. My officers are combing this city, block by block, in search of their daughter." Drawing from his own experience, Agent Donovan comforted the parents as he greeted them.

"Hello Mr. and Mrs. Wilkes. I'm agent Brian Donavan. I want you to know that we're working diligently to bring your daughter home."

Peyton's head hung low, her arms folded. Hot tears streamed down her face, as she grieved for her baby. Her feet felt like lead, and she found it difficult to walk. Gil assisted her, gently moving her along with the touch of his hand, in the small of her back. Agent Donovan reached out his hand to assist her along with Gil. She was taken to a comfortable seat.

"I know you're upset and you're in shock right now, but I really need to ask you some questions about what's happened in the last few days. You must cooperate fully, so we can quickly bring the baby home safely. We need to work fast because, as you know, the more time passes, the less of a chance we'll have of bringing the baby h..." He watched as Peyton sobbed at the thought of her baby not coming home. He stopped short, not finishing his sentence. It was only causing more pain, and he wanted her to keep her faith.

"Mrs. Wilkes. I'm going to need you to be strong for your daughter. Do you think you can do that for me?" With her body trembling, she nodded her head. As questioning was about to begin, lead detective Sheppard stood by and recorded the interview. He would participate as well.

"First thing I need to ask is, when was the first time that you were contacted by Delilah Castellucci?" Gil, still holding on to his wife, said,

"About a month ago; my assistant can give you the exact date. She came by my office with a couple of her men, requesting that I perform a risky surgery on her, but I refused. I thought that was the end of it until she showed up at my daughter's christening a week later. She didn't say much, but she gave my wife a threatening gift."

"What type of threatening gift?"

"I'll get them for you," Gil said as he stood to go and retrieve the items.

"It was an old doll with a porcelain face that had been shattered. A surgeon's scalpel was taped to its chest. The letter said to watch out for my family, and it had the initials *D. C.* I assumed it was from Delilah Castellucci. I still have it. They also shipped Mr. Sam's money clip by courier to our home as if we didn't already know they had taken him. Gil went into his home office, got the items, and returned and handed them to the investigators. They were taken for evidence. "I'll have them sent to the lab," said Detective Sheppard. "Okay, continue Mr. Wilkes," Agent Donovan said.

"I hadn't heard from her until they contacted me about Mr. Sam. I was told to cooperate, or they would kill him. I was told not to contact the police. Looking back now, it was a foolish thing to do, but we love Mr. Sam. The thought of anything happening to him was too much. When I heard him screaming in the background, I knew I had to do something to help him. I just wanted him back alive, and that evil woman out of our lives. That was the main reason I refused the surgery. I was afraid that I would be blamed if the surgery didn't turn out the way she wanted. Given the rumors of her husband's ties to organized crime, I wanted to wash my hands of the entire situation. She wouldn't let it go. She demanded that I perform the surgery, and she would release my friend. I did as she asked. Not only did she not release him, but she also stole our child." Gil burst into a crying fit. "If I had listened to Hal, our child would still be here. He warned me to notify the police. I thought I could handle things on my own. Now our baby and Mr. Sam are missing. And Clara; how could she betray our family? She stood right here with us, and she was working with the kidnappers all along."

"Our men are going over her room right now. That area will be inaccessible to the family as we continue our investigation do you understand?"

"Okay"

"Now, Hal, he's the head of your security team, right?"

"Yes"

"And when did you notify him of the kidnapping?"

"I notified him yesterday."

"Where was he when the nanny left with the child?"

"I'm not sure. I just know if he was here, he wouldn't have allowed her to leave, especially with the knowledge of threats, and Mr. Sam's kidnapping."

"What can you tell me about the men at the clinic?"

"Honestly, they looked like the classic mafia guys from the movies. They were huge Italian men, dressed in business suits. She called one of them Giovanni. He appeared to be the head. The other guy's name was Frankie. There were others outside the clinic, but I didn't get to see them. They were in large black SUVs."

"Do you own the building that houses the clinic?"

"Yeah"

"Do you have surveillance cameras at that location?"

"Yes, I do."

"We need the information of your security company. I'm sure there's plenty of footage of the men. We'll need that so the press can have images for the press release. Since Mrs. Castellucci is unconscious, perhaps finding these men will be a clue to finding your baby."

Gil provided the authorities with the information requested. All footage provided was processed from the day of the initial visit, then the day of the kidnapping. Detective Sheppard walked in interrupting the meeting, "Agent Donovan, the surveillance video from the church, and the Wilkes clinic are available. We have crystal clear images of all the suspects involved. We even have the men in the parking lot. The phone records of the nanny have been expedited and are available. Neither of the suspect's phones are tracking. We were, however, able to follow each signal, searching for any surveillance cameras, which coincided with the routes taken when the phones were tracking. We've determined where the hideout is. That location is being processed. But at the moment, no one is home. It appears the homeowners would often rent their homes to tourists using the online platform. We're checking to see who rented the home during the time of the kidnapping. That information should be available in a few minutes."

"Thank you, Detective," Agent Donovan said. He excused himself from the parents. He went into the part of the home where they had set up shop and downloaded the information on his laptop. Clara, Delilah, and her men's cell phones were linked together. Investigators noticed the phones were in constant contact. The timeline was a week before the kidnappings. Delilah had the Wilkes family under surveillance. She realized Clara was the nanny. She persuaded her to come on board with the promise of immediate citizenship and enough money to live anywhere she wanted. The opportunity seemed like a great one, and it was tempting. Clara's money troubles would be over, and she could live her dreams without having to work again. Clara jumped at the opportunity, and to seal the deal, she was given a ten-thousand-dollar cash down payment.

She was promised the rest once the child was delivered. Delilah and Clara's phones were in constant contact with Leonardo Puccini, also known as Lenny. And they were pinging off several towers in the Memphis area. They were able to track their whereabouts up until the phones stopped tracking near the Mississippi River. The only phone that was still active was Delilah's. Having the calls linked together, the investigators knew the extent of each player's involvement. After further checking Clara's phone records, they noticed that she'd been in contact with one security guard at the guard shack. This guard was fairly new. He was a fill-in from a temp agency. He was recently hired because one of the regular guards had to go on family leave. They tracked the security guard's phone with that of Lenny's, and they, too, had been involved in several texts and calls. Turns out he was a high school dropout. He had committed a few petty crimes as a teen. After being released into his mother's care, she threatened to put him out if he didn't go back to school or get a job. He sold drugs and worked part-time at the local grocery store until his twenty-first birthday. With an expunged record, he was able to get a job as a security guard.

Aaron Jackson is his name. Police went to the address associated with his employee record and cell phone bill. It was his mother's home. Detective Sheppard knocked on the door. He looked around the yard and noticed it was very well-groomed. A middle-aged biracial woman came to the door. She had a towel wrapped around her head and was wearing a robe. She noticed the badge on the detective's belt as well as his weapon. She exhaled as she knew somehow it involved her son. "What did he do this time?" she asked. "Ma'am, my name is Detective Sheppard. I'm with the Major Crimes division of Memphis. May I speak with you for a minute?" She looked around and noticed there was a squad car behind the detective's car with two police officers outside. "Is everything alright? I mean, is the boy okay?" "If you'll allow me to speak with you for a minute. I'll explain why I'm here." She backed away and

allowed Detective Sheppard inside. "What is it?"
"Excuse me, ma'am, I didn't get your name." I'm
Nancy Jackson. What's going on?"

"Do you have a son named Aaron Jackson?"

"Yes, I do. Is he okay?"

"As far as I know, he is. I'm looking for him. I
need to ask him some questions."

"About what," she asked. She unwrapped her
hair and blotted it to dry it. She then placed the
towel on her shoulders. The detective showed her a
photo of her son. "Is this Aaron Jackson your
son?"

"Yes, it is."

"Well, ma'am, your son works for a very
important family. Their child has been taken. We
believe he may have some information on the
kidnappers. We want to speak to him. Can you
please tell me where we can find him?"

"He recently rented a fancy new apartment on
the other side of town. I'm unsure of the address
because I've never been there, but I can give you

the name. My son hasn't mentioned anything to me about any kidnapping, so what would make you think he would know something about this?

"Ma'am, we're questioning all the staff members, not just your son. It's standard procedure. We want to see what he knows, if anything, and rule him out. Is there any way you can call him for me? Have him meet me here?"

"Yes, I can call him."

Do me a favor; don't tell him I want to speak with him. I don't want to scare him off. A child's life is at stake, and we really need his help in this case. Will you do that?"

"Yes, I will." Eager to help, the mother called her son. She made up a story of needing his help. The detective asked the officers in the squad car to move around the corner and descend upon him as soon as they noticed him. They pulled him over. He was driving a new pickup truck. He had a wad of cash on him and inside his vehicle. He was taken into custody. As a courtesy, the detective told his mother they had him in custody.

Out of fear that the child would die, and he would get the death penalty, he fully cooperated with authorities. He spoke of his involvement. He told of a visit he received from two large men. They wanted him to allow the nanny to leave the property without interference. Afterwards, they made subtle threats against him and his family if he didn't cooperate. He was paid off ahead of the job. Since he was kept out of the loop, all he had going for him was that he spoke with Lenny and Clara by phone. He didn't think he would be discovered for his betrayal. He immediately left his post when Clara left. He didn't hear from Lenny anymore.

There was a media circus outside the home. Kali Thompson was reporting live as updates were slowly coming in about the case. Key information was kept hidden from the public to maintain the investigation's integrity. The only information given was to help locate the missing child and bring her other captors to justice. The media was camped out near the hospital, trying to get answers about Delilah's condition. Her health worsened, and she remained in a comatose state. The search was on for Samuel. A full investigation was underway into Dante Castellucci's life, and the Feds were monitoring his activities closely, looking for any signs of the baby.

A *Silver Alert* was issued for Samuel, and his face was plastered over the media outlets. Given what Gil shared with authorities about the violence of the kidnappers, they were afraid it was more of a recovery effort.

The Following Day....

It was nearing eight-thirty in the morning. A local sanitation crew was going about their workday. Taking a shortcut to get to the homes on the next street, the driver went through the alley. They noticed a large bulky object blocking their right-of-way. Not wanting to damage his work vehicle, the driver swerved to miss the object, but he still couldn't get past it. He pulled the air brakes and hopped down out of his vehicle to move the debris. The two workers on the back of the truck were curious about why they'd stopped in the alley. They jumped down from their steps and went to the front of the truck. When the driver walked closer, he noticed it was an elderly man who had been severely beaten. He appeared to be dead. The driver was afraid to touch him because he had seen the crime shows. He didn't want to contaminate the possible murder scene. He took his cell phone from his front pocket and called 911. He also notified his dispatcher of what they had discovered. The dispatcher sent a field supervisor out. She also sent another truck to help finish their route. She knew the police would hold up the crew as witnesses. While they waited, the driver noticed the man's eyes twitching and thought he saw his stomach slowly rise and fall. "Is he alive?" One of the men asked the driver.

"Nah, I don't think so. Sometimes dead people get that last breath out. Doesn't seem like he's been here that long" the driver said.

"He moved again!"

"Man, that's just your eyes playing tricks on you. That man is as dead as a doorknob. The man began to moan.

"Oh shit, he *is* alive!" the driver said. He called 911 again and told them the man was still alive, and they needed to send paramedics. The police began arriving, and the sanitation crew stood off to the side. After answering questions, they were released and allowed to continue their workday. The badly injured man was barely clinging to life.

He had no identification on him. It was Samuel Banks. He was immediately taken to the hospital.

After stabilizing him, officials began the task of identifying him. An officer was sent to the hospital to obtain fingerprints, and a sketch was made of him just in case they needed it. Anyone working with children, including volunteers, must consent to a federal background check and submit their fingerprints. Since Samuel volunteered at the elementary school, his fingerprints were already on file with the Memphis state police. His children, who had been notified of his abduction, had flown into the city of Memphis with police protection. They stayed at a local hotel instead of their father's home and awaited news about their father. When his identity was officially verified, his children were notified. Relieved that he was alive, they were allowed to visit him at his bedside.

By now, everyone in America had heard about the kidnapping of baby Grace and Samuel. They were aware of Delilah's involvement. It was on the local and national news. Whenever one would log on to their online accounts, it was flooded with stories and images of Delilah and her crew. Her husband, Dante Castellucci, was under heavy scrutiny. The heat was on the Castellucci organization, and Dante wasn't happy about it. After repeatedly denying any involvement in the kidnappings through his team of attorneys, he launched a damage control campaign. First, he needed to get to the bottom of what really happened and who was involved. His driver took him to his beloved building. His trusted crew of friends were there along with Frankie, Lenny, and Giovanni. Giovanni and Frankie were trying to explain the details of Delilah's plans. For the most part, they were assigned to her, and Dante wanted answers. Dante looked on with dark and piercing eyes. He instilled a sense of fear in the hearts of all who knew him among his circle of henchmen. He'd killed many a man while taking over their territories and making a name for himself in the underground world. He'd managed to elude his enemies and the many police investigations that resulted in no charges being brought against him. He stayed under the radar of local and federal law enforcement agencies. He kept his hands clean while others carried out hits for him. All was quiet on the home front until Delilah's stunt.

The men were gathered outside on the terrace. The yard was dimly lit. Dante's face glowed in the bright moonlit sky. He looked towards Giovanni for answers.

"What do you mean by bringing this heat on me, Giovanni?"

"Boss, it was Mrs. C. She said she needed us to escort her for a gig. You were the one who told us to take care of her boss, so we did as we were told. She made it seem like the job was to be done with your approval. It was supposed to be a simple gig. We were told to hold the old man until her surgery was over, but Lenny and the boys beat him and dumped his body. That's when they went for the baby."

"Is that it? Is that all you have to say for yourself? You're just going to blame someone else? Giovanni, how many times have I told you that no matter what you've heard or what you think you know about me, I don't do business across state lines unless I give the order?"

"But Boss, this didn't have anything to do with the Castellucci side of the business."

"Giovanni, every time you make a move on behalf of my wife, you must run it by me."

"Boss, we didn't know. Mrs. C. made us think you wanted us to help her. She said you were busy and should not be disturbed. I didn't want to question her about it, and I didn't want to insult you or her by bringing it to your attention. I swear I thought you already knew."

"I don't conduct my business that way. I'm no criminal. What makes you think I'm into kidnapping? Have you ever known me to hurt anyone? I'm a legitimate businessman. You've never seen me murder, kidnap, or harm anyone. You guys have managed to kidnap a famous physician's child, kill his help, and bring this heat down on me. Now, all my transactions must cease. I'm not allowed to conduct any business. The feds are swarming all over us like flies on shit, and you have nothing else to say, but you thought I was in on this bullshit. Where's this kid?"

Lenny was afraid to speak up. Although it's true that they'd never seen Dante kill anyone, it went without saying that he was behind a lot of shady dealings. They knew they were in trouble. They feared for their lives. Stumbling on broken words, Lenny said, "We...we have her and the nanny in a safe place."

"So, the baby is still alive."

"Yes, the baby and the nanny for now."

"What do you mean, for now?"

"Well, we didn't know what to do with them. Not until Mrs. C. could tell us what she wanted to be done. She got herself caught so we fled."

"From what I hear, you guys left her there."

"I went back for her. The cops were on the way. I couldn't get her to the vehicle in time," Giovanni said. Frankie left me to deal with her alone. Frankie left, and the driver was about to leave me, too. Mrs. C. was fresh out of surgery. She was hooked up to all these contraptions. I didn't want her to die. I knew the authorities would take her to the hospital. We couldn't risk staying. We would've gotten caught. We didn't kill the doc or his people. The police were going to find out it was her anyway. Even if we had killed him, there was no way of us knowing who he'd already told about the job. I decided to give her a chance to live. I didn't want her to die."

Dante said, "You left my wife there to save your own ass."

"There was nothing we could do," Giovanni reiterated.

"Boys, you've fucked up. And about the kid, I don't want anything to happen to her. If that kid dies, it will be the end of my business. I don't need that kind of shit on my conscious, and I don't need the heat. I have multimillion-dollar deals in the works, and now no one will touch me due to all of this unwanted attention. I want the kid returned to her family."

"But boss, how are we going to manage that?"

"I don't give a damn how you get her back; I want it done. I want my name cleared so the feds can back off, and my business can resume. Also, I need you to get rid of your cell phones. Anything that can connect you to both kidnappings, get rid of it immediately."

"It's already done, Mr. Castellucci. That's the first thing we did when we realized the police were closing in. We left them in the Mississippi River."

"You need to get burners. Give the numbers to the boys. They'll be able to contact you without the police knowing about it. Once the kid is returned, I will have to let you guys go. I can't have you on the payroll any longer. It's too risky. Now go on and do as I say. Once the transaction is complete, you'll be compensated, and you'll have to find new gigs. If you keep your mouths closed, I'll protect you."

Dante looked toward Benny and Tommy with a simple head. No words were needed.

CHAPTER SIX

A week later, Delilah was still unconscious. A continuous live video feed went from her room to the FBI. Authorities kept a vigil by her bedside. Knowing the end of the road had come for Delilah, they feared her accomplices would get rid of the baby in an effort to remain anonymous. They were desperate for answers.

Hearing the news, Delilah's mother flew in to be by her side. Before being allowed in to see her, she was questioned by authorities. She was taken into a private room by agents. "Ma'am, I'm agent Brian Donovan with the Federal Bureau of Investigations, and this is agent Cathy Bishop of the Tennessee State Bureau. May we have a word with you?"

"But I want to see my daughter, she needs me."

"You'll be allowed to see her but first we must speak."

"Look I don't know anything about the kidnappings, so I wouldn't have any answers for you. There's nothing I can say that'll help your case. Now let me see my daughter." The feisty middle-aged lady tried to move past the two agents. They successfully blocked her path.

"Ma'am, please cooperate with us; it won't take long," said Agent Donovan.

Look, I'm just as concerned about the baby as everyone else. If you let me see my daughter, perhaps I can get some answers."

"Can you tell us about her state of mind or the motivation behind her actions? Has she always been like this? I mean, we know her in the public arena, but what was she like in private?"

"Look, my daughter was a happy child. She was friendly and easygoing. She was loved by all her peers. She's very bright and extremely beautiful. Not only was she beautiful, but she was also a talented actor, singer, and performer. She was so good that she began doing TV commercials at an early age. She was cast in many small parts, but she soon began to get bigger roles. Before we knew it, she was a famous star. It all happened so fast. She married the man of her dreams, and she lived a happy life."

"Does it surprise you that your daughter is being accused of kidnapping and other crimes?"

"Agent Donovan, is it? I never would've thought that my daughter could remotely commit these crimes. I had to come to see for myself and get my own answers. This sounds nothing like her"

"So, you're saying you never saw this coming?

"No mother could predict this."

"So, there were no warning signs that she was having difficulties, no emotional changes or anything?"

"She had been having some issues after several surgeries left her severely disfigured, but I never thought she would take such drastic measures."

"From what we're hearing from her victims, he was forced to perform surgery while her crew held them hostage. From what we gather, she had the nanny kidnap the child. We're also looking into the untimely deaths of both her former surgeons. It can't be a coincidence that they're both dead only months apart after her surgeries. The motive is becoming clearer, but we want to gain some insight into her mindset. Had she ever behaved this way before?"

"As I told you, she had a great childhood, a great career, and a wonderful marriage until the surgeries. She tried going to several other doctors, but they all turned her down. She could've been distraught. I know she was suffering inside. It sounds like the actions of a painfully desperate person who's suffering from a mental breakdown. The kind of emotional ordeal that causes women to take drastic measures to get what they want. Some steal babies and take them as their own to get their mates to love them. They do not care who they hurt in the process. It appears she may have been detached from reality, to even think this plan would work. Now a lot of people have been hurt. My heart breaks for the families who are being affected by her actions, however, I'm still her mother, and as her mother, I'm concerned about her mental and physical well-being. So please; may I see my daughter now?'

"Yes, ma'am. You can see her. We'll escort you."

Her mother was allowed several brief supervised visits. The visits were monitored and recorded. She camped out at the hospital waiting for her daughter to regain consciousness, not just for her well-being, but she too wanted to help find the child.

There were armed agents outside of Samuel's hospital room. Authorities were waiting for him to regain his strength so that perhaps he could tell them more about his abductors. He was in fair condition but was still unable to talk. He was getting better daily.

Samuel- I opened my eyes today. I realize I'm in the hospital. I blacked out after another round of severe beatings. I thought for sure that when I opened my eyes this time, I would be facing my creator. I'm okay, well I'm alive. I can't open my mouth. My jaw is wired shut. I have a patch over one eye, I'm wrapped tight like a mummy. Sam Jr. is here. I want to tell him not to look so worried. But his back is turned to me. Turn around son. Talk to me. I can hear you. My daughter is crying. She doesn't know I can see and hear her. Pam, stop crying. I'm here. Wait a minute, who is that young man with his arms around my daughter? I've never met him before. Is that her boyfriend? She never told me she was seeing anyone. Where's Eli? I don't see him. Oh, come on, Sam Jr., look at me. Perhaps if I make a sound, he'll see that I'm awake."

Samuel lets out a loud groaning noise. Pam looked up from her crying. She flew from her friend's arms and ran to her father's side. "Jr,

Dad's awake. Get the nurse, Andy!" she said to her friend. Sam Jr. was standing next to his father's bed filled with hope. He could see a slight smile on his father's face. Samuel tried reaching for his son. Sam Jr. took his hand, held it, and gently placed it back by his father's side. "Welcome back, Dad. You gave us quite a scare. You're pretty banged up. They did quite a number on you. Looks like you're going to be okay." Sam Jr. kissed his father's forehead and then moved out of his sister's way. She wanted to get closer to him. Knowing he was fragile; she couldn't give him the hug she wanted. She simply did as her brother did. She held his hand and kissed his forehead. "Oh, Daddy, you had me so worried." The nurse rushed into the room with Eli and Andy following. She checked Samuel's vitals and did what she could to make him comfortable. She tried communicating with him. There was a respiratory intubation placed in his nose since his jaw had been wired shut. This was so he could breathe. He turned his head to look at the nurse. "Mr. Banks, I'm Nurse Margorie. Are you feeling okay?" Samuel blinked his eyes and moaned. He nodded his head once. He tried moving his mouth. His lips moved and he spoke, but his words were difficult to make out.

Samuel-They can hear me. Now I hope they can understand me. They know I'm awake. I just need them to know I'm in here and still in my right mind. I'm going to try again. This time I'm going to call my beloved daughter's name. Here it goes."

Samuel turned his head, and his eye sought out his daughter's. He fixed his gaze directly towards her and whispered. "Pam,"

"Yes, Daddy, I'm here," she said. She took his hand. "I'm here." Her light brown face and tight eyes lit up.

"I...I love you," he said.

"Oh, Daddy," she said with a sigh of relief and laughter. "I love you too." They continued their reunion and comforted their father.

After the media caught wind of Samuel's safe return, it was reported on the news. Out of fear of reprisal, Samuel was removed from the hospital and taken to a safe location. He was given a pseudonym for his protection. His children remained at his bedside.

Peyton had a strong Christian faith. Her church family rallied around her, and Gil lent their support. They held prayer vigils and passed out fliers of the baby. The couple's parents and her pastor had pretty much camped out within the home. As agents came and went, Peyton, sat on the sofa holding Grace's blanket. Her mother, Mrs. Brockington, was sitting next to her. With a missing granddaughter, and seeing the pain her daughter was experiencing, she felt useless as a mother. Throughout Peyton's life, she'd faced a few issues of which she was able to comfort her daughter, but this ordeal was taking its toll on not only her but the entire family.

As they sat on the sofa watching authorities and awaiting word of the baby's safety, Peyton began to have a severe anxiety attack. Her mother held her, rocking her, trying to calm her. She, too, began to break under the pressure. Gil's mother joined the women as well. Peyton's father, Mr. Brockington seeing his daughter in distress, grabbed his cane and stood to his feet. He hurried over to her. He gently pushed his wife and everyone out of the way. Peyton fell into her father's arms.

"I'm here baby girl," he said as hot tears streamed from his eyes.

"Daddy, it hurts so badly. My baby is gone. I miss her, I need her. Help me, Daddy, help me."

"Baby girl, it's going to be alright. Trust me. She's going to be okay, and everything will work out. I promise you."

"But how can you say that, Daddy?"

"Look at me, Princess. Have I ever let you down? Have I ever said anything to you that hasn't come true? When I told you that you would pass the bar did you? When I said you would give me a granddaughter, even when you thought it was impossible, didn't it happen? How many times have I told you something would happen, and although you doubted me, it still came to pass? Well, believe me when I say this: Grace is coming home, and she will come home unharmed. You have to believe it. Hold on to hope baby girl. Do you believe me?" Peyton looked at her father with trust and said,

"Yes, Daddy. I believe you. But the pain is unbearable. Just thinking of what evil could be happening to her. Does she miss me? Is she being mistreated? Is she afraid? All these thoughts keep running through my head. I can't turn them off." The rest of the family surrounded them, and they all embraced one another. They gathered together to pray.

Once Peyton was a little calmer, she was offered a sedative that had been prescribed. Her doctor knew she would probably need it. Silvia brought a glass of water and the sedative. Peyton refused the pill.

"I have to remain alert. I can't sit around here drugged up, while my baby is out there with some gangster thugs. She needs me. I won't rest until I can hold my child in my arms again."

"I'm going to place it right here just in case," said Silvia. Silvia moved out of their way. She busied herself by bringing beverages to the agents in the home and cleaning behind them. She was just as worried about the baby. She silently prayed as she went about her chores. She was relieved to know that Samuel was going to be okay, but for her safety as well as Samuel's, she wasn't allowed to see him.

A few more days had passed, and word came that Delilah was awake. Peyton felt a sense of urgency. She pleaded with the authorities to allow her to leave, so she could visit with her, but she wasn't allowed to see Delilah. The police didn't want to lose any chance of getting information from her. Her husband Dante heard she was conscious. He rushed to Memphis to speak with her, but not before his attorneys went on the record again, speaking with authorities and news media on why he was making the visit.

"We've received word that my client's wife, Delilah Castellucci is alert. Just like the rest of you, my client will be seeking answers as to why his wife would commit such a heinous crime in which he had no prior knowledge or involvement. His main concern is to speak with Mrs. Castellucci about the safe return of the Wilkes' missing child. We hope that she gets the help she desperately needs, and that swift justice is brought upon all involved."

Dante was in Memphis. The media stood at the hospital grounds, trying to get a story from him or anyone they could glean information from. Dante slipped past them as his attorneys again spoke with the media on their client's behalf. Kali Thompson, who was still following the case, asked Dante's lead attorney Jon Cox, "Mr. Cox, we've now known that Mrs. Castellucci is awake, and it looks as if she will have to answer for her alleged crimes. Will your firm represent her when she's formally charged?"

"My firm represents Mr. Dante Castellucci and his interests alone. As I said before, Mrs. Castellucci allegedly committed these crimes without our client's knowledge. Mr. Castellucci is an upstanding member of society. He's a great and honorable man. He's risen above the salacious lies, and stories of him having ties to organized crime. We're unsure of why these personal attacks have been aimed at my client's reputation over the years, but all have proven to be false. He's never been arrested for a crime. He doesn't have so much as a parking ticket. He has a spotless record. He's here to get answers so that perhaps he can help the family. No parent should have to suffer as this family is now. Mr. Castellucci and I are truly heartbroken. Our thoughts are with the Wilkes family, and we pray for the baby's safe return to her loved ones. That is if Delilah Castellucci will cooperate with authorities."

After answering a few more questions, Dante's attorney escorted him into the hospital. Dante had gone ahead, and he was speaking with doctors about his wife. He was also questioned by the same agents who questioned his mother-in-law. He informed them that their relationship was strained, due to the botched surgeries, and they hadn't been spending much time together as a couple. He had no way of knowing of her whereabouts and had no clue she would be orchestrating such a calculated plan. After being questioned, he was allowed to go in to see her. The agents were somewhat convinced. They'd been watching and monitoring his activities for days. After digging into his background and his phone records; they couldn't find any link to him or any of the suspected players during the times of the kidnappings. The agents followed him into the room to monitor them. A nurse was standing by Delilah's bedside checking her vitals. She was blocking Dante's line of sight to his wife. When she was finished, she moved to the other side of the room. Dante walked closer to her bedside. He could see the slight scarring from the surgery. He couldn't help but stare at her for a few minutes. He began studying her face. She had gone from being the most beautiful woman he's ever seen, to being disfigured with marred facial features. But this face; this woman, he didn't know. Although her face was a little swollen, he could see the great job of the skilled surgeon. She didn't look like she did before the botched surgeries. Her appearance was better; far smoother. Her nose was straightened; her mouth was no longer crooked, and her cheeks were rosy and in their proper place. He was amazed at the outcome of the surgery. She finally got what she wanted but at the expense of others. She noticed him standing there. With her frail hand, she reached for him. He moved in closer. With a hoarsened voice, she whispered,

"Dante, I'm so glad you're here. What do you think? Do you like it?" Not wanting to be too hard on her, he said,

"Darling, you look amazing, but what have you done?"

"I fixed it, babe. Now you can love me again. We can be together again."

"And we will darling, but please tell me, why did you do this?"

"I had to baby. I needed you to love me again. It was difficult living without your love. There was no other way."

"But darling, I've always loved you. You didn't have to do this. Besides, you're hurting a lot of people. The parents of the little one want answers."

"She won't be harmed. I'll return the baby. I only wanted him to do the surgery. I didn't mean for anyone to get hurt. I'm sorry sweetheart. I did it for us."

One of the agents named Cathy Bishop, who has an infant of her own, was getting impatient so she interrupted the conversation,

"Mrs. Castellucci, where's the baby?" It was apparent to everyone watching that the harsh tone in her voice made Delilah uncomfortable. Dante looked around at the agent and said, "Ma'am, please don't speak to my wife in that tone. Can't you see how sickly she is? With all due respect, you're not going to receive answers by yelling at her. Allow me to handle this."

Delilah refused to answer Agent Bishop. Her focus remained on her husband.

"I'm ready to go home. Will you take me home Dante?"

"Yes, my love, but please, tell me who has the baby? We need to get her home to her parents. As soon as you tell me where she is, I'll take you home right away." Delilah smiled. She enjoyed the thought of her husband taking her home. She was still feeling loopy. She was rambling on underneath her breath, but her words weren't audible.

Agent Bishop, still thinking about her daughter, was losing her patience. She couldn't imagine someone kidnapping her child. The mere thought of it upset her even more. She felt they were losing valuable time by coddling Delilah, and it was getting on her last nerve. As much as she tried to remain professional, the rage within caused her to blurt out,

"Where's the baby, Mrs. Castellucci? Tell us where the child is. We need to return her to her family!"

She continued raising her voice and demanding answers. Delilah was getting upset. She began to shut down. The excitement of the moment was too much for her. Her blood pressure spiked. Her eyes blinked uncontrollably, and then they rolled into the back of her head. She slipped into a coma. The nurse tried everything she could while signaling for help. As doctors poured in to help Delilah, the agent was removed from the room, as well as from the case. She was placed on immediate suspension for losing her patience and compromising the investigation.

CHAPTER SEVEN

Now that Delilah was back in a coma, the authorities felt they would never get the answers they needed. They aggressively searched for her henchmen. Also, since the agents themselves witnessed the conversation between Dante and Delilah, they were sure that Dante played no part in the baby's abduction. They were convinced his wife acted without his knowledge. Dante denied knowing any of the men who'd assisted Delilah in her crimes except for Giovanni.

He informed them that Giovanni served as his driver and was assigned other small jobs for Dante. Even still he denied knowing of his whereabouts and wasn't privy to their plans. All men involved in the kidnappings were on the Castellucci payroll. Dante explained that he had thousands of people who were employed with the Castellucci Corporation, not to mention all the businesses he owned around the US. He couldn't rightfully know every employee who works for the company or their daily deeds. He continued to express that he would fully cooperate with law enforcement and gave Giovanni's cell phone number to the authorities. Of course, he was aware that they already had that information, but he had to make it appear that he was helping. He told them to check with human resources for information on the rest of the men in the surveillance video. Dante had already relocated Giovanni and Frankie to safe houses. He had Lenny stationed at the hotel with Clara. He knew the police wouldn't find them. He had his own plans for the men.

Dante exited the room. He was met by his mother-in-law, who was upset with him. She was allowed in to see her daughter before all the commotion, but she had to leave to make room for Dante.

He loved her dearly and treated her as if she were his own mother, even though they were closer to the same age. He watched as she nervously walked the floor of the hospital. She tried to fix her messy graying bun. She was dressed nicely, wearing a neat floral dress she'd purchased from Neiman Marcus. Since word of her daughter came to her, she refused to eat or sleep. He went over to her. "Mama Sophie," he said, opening his arms to her.

She fell in his arms and sobbed. She regained her composure and said, "I blame you for this. You promised me you would take care of my daughter. You promised her grandparents, but most of all, you made a promise to her. You are complicit in this crime. You may not have helped her do this, but you're the reason she felt desperate enough to do so. She wanted your love, and you all but abandoned her. I sat there, day in, and day out, watching her cry her eyes out with the hopes you'd come to love her again, but no, you couldn't keep your promise. What happened to your vows to love her for better or worse, in sickness and in health?

If the shoe were on the other foot, she would've stood by your side. Your damn reputation and your appearance were so important to you, that you left your young wife hanging. Since she no longer looked the part, she didn't fit into your world anymore. Rejection is very painful for a woman, especially when everyone walks away. She understood her agents walking away, perhaps even her so-called friends, but you Mr. Dante Castellucci, were all she had aside from me. You failed her. I'm so glad I was here to help her during this difficult time"

"Mama Sophie, I'm so sorry. You're right; I was being a bit selfish, but I was suffering too. I tried, in the beginning, to remain by her side, but she was so self-conscious that she began to push me away. No matter how I tried to convince her of my love, she refused to believe me. The relationship became strained. She kept insisting that I take her out in public. I knew if I'd done that, the public would've noticed her marred appearance, and they were bound to attack her in the media. That would've been even more difficult for her. She would've become the latest joke, a meme, and the laughingstock of America. All the beautiful works and everything she's worked for over the years would no longer matter to her fans. Instead, she'd be remembered for her horrid appearance. Since they don't know her personally, they'll cover that story, instead of the beautiful woman we both know and love. She was beautiful inside and out, but she had become someone I no longer recognized. Not only had her appearance changed, but she changed emotionally, and I wasn't equipped to deal with it. One minute she embraced me by allowing me into her space, then the next, she seemed to push me away. I didn't know what to do. I asked her to seek professional help. I even offered to go to marriage counseling. I told her if the marriage was going to work, we would have to work together but she continued obsessing over her appearance. I must admit I couldn't seem to get used to looking at her in that state, but I felt it was only temporary. I was optimistic that we would find the right surgeon at the right time to perform her corrective surgery. She lost hope and began drinking heavily, doping up on pain meds, and using cocaine. I was losing her all the way around, so yeah, I checked out of the marriage. I threw myself into my work.

Mama Sophie, you must know that I love my wife. I didn't feel comfortable coming to my mother-in-law as a coward, with my tail tucked between my legs; a guy who couldn't hold his marriage together. I was supposed to be the strong one. She looked up to me for help. I wanted help for her; for us. It just wasn't going to happen. I regret she felt the need to carry out this crime. Now this will forever be a part of her legacy."

Sophia stood listening to her son-in-law. She knew he loved Delilah and was telling the truth about her daughter. She was aware that Delilah was unstable in her advanced deteriorated state. She exhaled and motioned for a comforting hug.

"I know you're right son," she said. "I guess I need somebody to blame. I wish you'd come to me. Perhaps we could've made a joint effort to provide the help she so desperately needed. Now it may be too late." Dante continued to console her.

The Wilkes and Brockington family were watching the news. They were holding on to hope that they would be given answers soon. It had been nine grueling days. Peyton pulled herself away from the rest of the family for a little privacy and she wanted time to pray. Believing her baby would be returned, she continued to pump daily. Because she hadn't eaten much, she could feel her body wasn't producing as much milk as before. She sobbed as the milk trickled from her breast. Having feelings of despair, she removed the pump, barely cleaned her breast, and slid on the floor in a fetal position. She cried until there were no more tears. She felt she was in a trance. She just laid there, too weak to move.

A sense of calm and peace flooded her soul. In a euphoric state, she felt her body being lifted from the floor onto her bed. She couldn't understand what was happening, but she was no longer in pain, nor was she afraid. When she opened her eyes, nobody was there. She could still feel a peaceful presence in her room. Somehow, she knew things would be okay. She sat on the edge of her bed. She took her bible from the nightstand and went into her daughter's room to read it in her rocking chair. The same chair she uses to feed her baby. Although the room had been worked over with a fine-tooth comb by the authorities, she took a blanket and one of the teddy bears Gil brought for Grace and settled into the chair. As soon as she opened her bible, it happened to fall on a page of chapter sixty, in the book of Isaiah. It was God's word that was given to his people promising that he would bring their children home. She knew it was a sign that Grace was coming home soon. She read a few more scriptures until she was calmer. Afterwards, she showered and then rejoined her family. She kept the experience to herself. In expectation of her baby's return, she asked Silvia to prepare her a small meal, so she could replenish her body and produce more milk.

The television was on. It was time for the nightly news. They were replaying his attorney's footage recorded earlier that day. An image of Dante flashed on the television screen. His face seemed to jump out at her. She tried reading his facial expression. She was eager to speak with him. Without telling anyone in her family or the police, she planned on meeting him personally. If he was a fraud, she felt she would be able to sense it. Her only problem was the authorities wouldn't allow her to travel alone, especially since they weren't sure of all Delilah's accomplices. None of the family members or staff was considered safe until everyone involved was captured.

Peyton researched Dante Castellucci. She reached out to his team of attorneys, and she left her contact information with them. She informed them that she wanted to speak with him personally. At the advice of his attorneys, he was told not to speak with her directly. When she was given the news, she pleaded her case but was met with the same answers. She wasn't deterred. She went to bed with hope in her heart.

The following morning her cell phone rang. It was Dante. He was aware of the probability the call was being monitored.

"Hello," Peyton answered in a soft voice.

"Hello Mrs. Wilkes. This is Dante Castellucci. I was told you wanted to speak with me."

Peyton breathed a sigh of relief. Dante knew it was only right to give this innocent mother, who had done no wrong, a chance to speak her mind, even if it was to criticize him or his wife. Peyton's voice was not at all what he expected. She was sweet and soft and very polite.

"Good morning Mr. Castellucci. I thank you so much for returning my call. I was told that you wouldn't be speaking with me."

"Mrs. Wilkes, this matter is far too important to let someone else handle it on my behalf."

"Thank you. I wanted to plead with you, sir. If there is anything you know about where I can find my baby, whether she is safe or not, would you please help me? I'm dying inside. This pain is so unbearable. She's my only child. She's not even six months old. She needs me. Please, if there's any information that you have that could lead me to my child, let me know." Feeling sorry for her Dante responded,

"Mrs. Wilkes, I want to extend my deepest, heartfelt, apology for the pain you're going through. Trust me when I tell you, I was in no way involved in the kidnapping of your sweet baby girl. I'm at a loss for words as to why my wife chose to take these actions, to harm your family, in such a vile manner."

"Thank you, Mr. Castellucci. I would like to meet you and talk to you face to face if I could."

Dante went silent.

"Are you still here?" Peyton asked.

"Yes, I'm here."

"Can you do that for me?" Dante exhaled.

"That's the least I can do. When would you like to meet?

"As soon as possible," she said softly.

"Would you like for me to come to your home, or will we meet in a place of your choosing?"

"If you don't mind, can you come to my home? I'm not allowed to leave without police protection. Besides, I'd like to be home in case there's a change in my daughter's case."

"I'll speak with my attorneys and see what can be arranged," he said.

"Thank you very much, Mr. Castellucci."

Peyton ended the call. Dante was taken aback by her kindness. She wasn't accusing him nor was she showing anger towards him. She was a desperate mother who loved and missed her baby. Dante couldn't understand how she could remain so calm. He definitely wanted to have her child returned to her. He spoke with his attorneys, and again, they informed him not to involve himself personally with the case or the Wilkes. He ignored their advice urging them to see things his way. With this meeting, he would prove once and for all, that he really cared about the child and the family. Working together with them would further cause the public to look favorably on him, as he handled the damage control. He wanted all of this to go away. The following day, with his attorneys by his side, he went to the home. Peyton was eagerly awaiting his visit. She finally spoke with Gil about the visit. Although Dante had been cleared of any involvement, Gil was uneasy about having the reported criminal and husband of his child's abductor in his home. He, too, wanted answers, so he went along with the visit. After confiding in her husband about her plans, she went to the head agent in charge to let them know about Dante's visit. It would be allowed.

When Dante arrived at the home, he noticed news reporters everywhere. Helicopters were flying overhead trying to get a glimpse of the home. The place was crowded and crawling with police presence. He was feeling uneasy, but he knew the meeting had to take place; especially given his claims of innocence. His car was waved through the large wrought iron gate. Once he made it down to the home, he stepped out of the back of the vehicle. As he walked towards the entry door, he noticed a handful of Memphis Police officers lining the entrance. After being searched by agents, he was allowed to enter. On the other side of the door, he noticed Peyton. She was a vision of loveliness. He tried not to stare but he couldn't help but do so. With a warm greeting and a kiss on each cheek, she held both his hands in hers and said,

"Welcome to our home, Mr. Castellucci." He was taken aback by her sweet smile, her kind eyes, and her gentle spirit.

"Thank you for having me."

Gil, unimpressed with Dante, greeted him reluctantly.

"Mr. Castellucci," Gil said, emotionless.

"Mr. Wilkes, I presume? It's a pleasure meeting you."

"You'll excuse me if I'm not currently in the mood for pleasantries. Our child's life is at stake. She's out there somewhere, perhaps with some dangerous criminals. She's been gone going on the second week, and we're heartbroken." Peyton looked at her husband with pleading eyes.

"Honey, please, he's here to help." She gently slipped her hands inside Gil's, to calm his inner rage toward Dante.

"Mr. Castellucci, may I speak with you in private please?" She looked toward the agents. Her parents were looking on. She said to the agent in charge,

"I'd like to have a moment of privacy without interference from law enforcement, or attorneys. No recordings, please. Just he and I."

They were allowed a private meeting. She led the way up the grand staircase towards her daughter's nursery, while Dante followed. She exuded strength, grace, and kindness which he had never seen before in anybody. Especially for someone whose child was missing. When they were alone, Dante said,

"Mrs. Wilkes, I sincerely apologize for the pain you're going through. You see, my wife Delilah is a very sick woman. She hasn't been herself for quite some time. About two years ago she began having these surgeries against my wishes. Seems she wanted a part in a movie, and she thought it would be best for her career. She was very beautiful. Not a flaw in her in any way. There were major complications during the surgery, and her face was severely marred. She tried to go back for more surgeries, but it made matters worse. Needless to say, we were devastated. While I do love my wife, it took some time for me to get used to seeing her disfigured face. I tried to love and support her, but her mental state began to deteriorate. She blamed me for not loving her and turning my back on her. I encouraged her to seek counsel, but she wouldn't leave the house. She would only go out in public with scarves, head coverings, and shades. I still had a business to run. I couldn't sit in the house with her day in, and day out. Sure, I admit that I probably added to her pain. She felt abandoned. I was ill-equipped to handle this, so I threw myself into my work. I began avoiding her because our times together, seemed to turn confrontational. It was taking its toll on me. After a while, I just stopped going around as much; maybe once or twice a month if that. I'm sure she was hurting. I'm not in any way condoning what she did; I'm just trying to gather some insight into why she would take such drastic measures."

"Mr. Castellucci, I met your wife once, but I didn't know who she was. I really can't remember her all that much. She came to our baby's christening. She handed me a gift for my baby. At the time, I didn't know that she had already gone to my husband and asked for the surgery. Gil is considered one of the best plastic surgeons in the field. Your wife was under the impression that he could reverse the damages. According to my husband, seems there were major risk factors that wouldn't allow for a successful surgery. My husband feared that if she didn't like the results, he would be blamed so he refused. She wouldn't take no for an answer. That's when things changed. Not only is Mr. Sam, one of our beloved friends a victim, but my beautiful little Grace is gone. Your wife is unconscious, and we have no answers."

"Yeah, about that; she was awake, and I thought I could get through to her, but the agent got a little too rough with her. She relapsed. She's not doing well. Perhaps we can try again later, that is if she regains consciousness."

"May I show you something?" she asked him.

"Sure,"

Peyton began to show Dante pictures of the baby. These are photos of the day of her birth. I never thought I could have children. I never considered that I would. But this day was considered a miracle. This was one of the best days of my life. God saw fit for us to bring a beautiful child into this world. Surely, He didn't bless us with such a beautiful soul, only to have her snatched away from us. My heart is filled with love, my breasts are filled with milk. My arms are filled with an empty space where my daughter should be. She's still a nursing infant and she needs me. A stranger has my baby, and I can only imagine her confusion and fear. Look at these photos.

"This is our angel; she's my heart and soul. She's an innocent child Mr. Castellucci. She's done nothing to deserve this. These past couple of weeks have been excruciating for me and my husband. I feel as though my soul has been snatched from my body. My heart aches not knowing what's happening to my child.

My husband desperately tried to help your wife. He was looking out for her best interest when refusing to perform her surgery. For his efforts, he was abused, and so was our good friend Mr. Sam. Now to our baby, I'm afraid harm has either come or will come to her. So please, Mr. Castellucci, if you know anything. If you think you can get someone who knows your wife that could tell you something about my baby's whereabouts. Will you let me know?"

She reached out for his hands. She looked up at him desperately pleading her case. He studied her eyes, her warm face, and her lovely eyes. Dante thought, *"How can she smile when she's going through this ordeal when it was my wife who caused this pain. I was sure she would blame me, but she is so kind."* Wanting to solve her problem, he took her hands and said,

"I'm so sorry Mrs. Wilkes. Rest assured; I'll do everything within my power to find out what happened. I feel strongly that everything's going to be okay," he said with a slight, reassuring head nod. As they communicated telepathically, she knew at that moment, that her child would be returned safely. He had the answers she needed, and she sensed it. She knew that he knew more than he was letting on but refused to incriminate himself. Dante whispered,

"Trust me when I tell you this Mrs. Wilkes, I had absolutely nothing to do with these crimes. They were done without my knowledge."

"I believe you Mr. Castellucci, and I trust you when you say everything is going to be okay."

"Please get some rest ma'am," he said while gently but purposefully squeezing her hand, reassuring her that things were fine. Peyton wrapped her arms around him and held him for a few seconds. He returned the hug. Emotional energy transferred from her body to his. He softened from a hardened killer, into a considerate man at the moment. These two strangers, whose lives were forced together by an unfortunate event, brought them to this space. Now they were connected forever. He would never forget her.

In the tender moment, she taught him something he'd needed for now and for the future. People aren't mere pawns in his cruel game of life. Real people were hurting due to his actions. He briefly thought of all the families whose lives were negatively affected by his cruel actions. Children who lost their parents, and loved ones at his hands were suffering, pain that would last for years. He never considered until now, how his actions were affecting others and up until this moment, he hadn't given it much thought. He thought of his own parents and the negative effect the Venturi brothers had on them, and their neighborhood. He remembered the pain on his mother's face as she watched her husband and vice versa being abused. This family is now hurting and missing their child. Their only crime was falling victim to his wife.

He may not have had anything to do with this particular crime, but he was now reliving the crimes he had committed. Could he change? Should he change? Meeting Peyton Wilkes made him want to try. She'd given him a lot to think about on his plane ride home.

Before he left, Peyton gave him a picture of the baby. He was escorted away. On the flight home, he couldn't stop thinking about Peyton. Never had anyone moved him as much as this mother did. He wanted to protect her and her child. He looked at the baby's picture. He thought she was adorable. Although he wanted children, especially a son, Delilah had been so wrapped up in her career, that she never wanted any. His heart was breaking for this family. He was angry with his wife for more than just bringing heat to his name, but for harming this innocent family. Although she committed the crime, he still loved her. Seeing her in her new image caused his emotions to fluctuate. He didn't know what to think or feel, but he still cared for her deeply. If only they could've met Gil under better circumstances, things could've possibly gotten better between the two. But now, her life was in peril. Their relationship was bound to end due to her imminent death or with her in prison, possibly for life. He was upset with Lenny and Frankie, but he was even angrier with Giovanni, and he wanted him to pay. Once he was back in New York, he called his friend Lucio. Together, they would hash out the best plan for all involved.

CHAPTER EIGHT

Dante had Delilah's men followed. Benny tracked Giovanni while Nicky and Tommy followed the other two.

Giovanni's nerves were on edge. He was a bit fearful of what would happen to him now that Dante knew about the baby. Not only that, but he also knew deep down that he would seek retribution for leaving Delilah to fend for herself. It was common knowledge that he still loved his wife. Leaving her was totally unacceptable, not to mention it brought a lot of heat on Dante. He contemplated turning himself in to the police, but he knew that would mean certain death. He knew very little about Dante's criminal activities. Not even enough to give to the feds in exchange for protection. Dante intentionally kept it that way. He never talked about business among the underlings, and he talked in code when they were in his presence. The only thing Giovanni suspected, was whenever Dante had a dispute with someone, that person would later end up dead. He knew it was no coincidence. He tried laying low, but he felt he was being followed. He went out around two in the morning. That way he could tell for sure if he was being followed. He left his apartment in Jersey. He walked a little way down to a soda machine. Before he could make it to the corner, he noticed a dark sedan with headlights off moving slowly behind him as he walked. He pretended not to notice. He put his bill inside the machine and pulled out his drink; all the while, his left hand was on his weapon. He walked around the block hoping to lose whoever was trailing him or at least get a better look at the vehicle. He was followed back to his place. He went inside and turned out all the lights. He peered out the window. The car seemed to pull away with the headlights out. Sleep left him. He stayed awake the rest of the night. The next day, he was hungry. He looked down the street to the left, then to the right. The car was gone. He proceeded to walk to the store to get him something to eat. He monitored his surroundings closely, but he was distracted by a loud blast of a horn. Seems one driver pulled away from the curb cutting another driver off. He stopped in his tracks. His knees shook violently when he looked up and noticed Benny blocking him on the sidewalk. "Damn, Benny, you scared the shit outta me," he said, gripping his chest.

"Giovanni, we need the location of the baby."

"I know Boss sent you here to kill me?"

"What are you talking about? Mr. Castellucci is no killer. You, of all people, should know that. You've never seen him murder anyone, and you've worked for him for many years. He wants the baby's location to ensure her safe return to her parents. He needs all of this to be over so he can continue his life. You owe him that much because it was you who brought this heat on his name. So, tell us where the child is."

"When I tell you, you're going to kill me."

"You're being paranoid. Nobody's going to kill you. Quite the opposite; Mr. Castellucci wants to protect you. As you know, he protects his own. He's always seen to it that we all were taken care of. Not one of us has ended up dead or in prison. And do you want to know why that is? It's because he cares. He's a kind man and a fair one. We're like family to him. He wants me to look after you. That's why I've been following you. I've been protecting you from the cops. You're gonna have to leave the safe house and go underground for your protection.

The feds are after you, Frankie, and Lenny. Your names and faces are all over the news. You're on the FBI's most wanted list. He wants to keep you guys out of prison."

"Yeah, but I heard about your work. The streets talk. Everyone knows you're a hired hitman for Boss. It goes without saying."

"How many times do I have to tell you I'm no killer? Besides, I'm not even armed. Wanna check me?"

Giovanni wanted to check him, but he decided to trust him for the time being. He shook his head and said, "Nah, I believe you."

"I'm so glad we got that out of the way. We need this heat to die down. So, tell me, where's the kid?"

"We have her hidden away in a hotel along with the Nanny. I'll get them on the phone for you."

Giovanni called Frankie's burner. After he answered, Giovanni gave the phone to Benny. Frankie gave Benny their location. After chatting with Frankie, he gave Giovanni his cell phone and walked away. Giovanni rushed away, heading in the opposite direction. He was relieved that his life had been spared. He didn't notice Benny had doubled back. A quick double-tap to the back of the head, and he was dead. Benny left, and immediately, a large, dark van pulled alongside his body. Three men got out and quickly loaded Giovanni's body in the van. Nobody saw a thing.

Benny called Tommy, who was following Lenny.

"Hey Tommy, what do you have on Lenny?"

"He's been going in and out of that old motel room. He's been buying things for the baby, and, I suppose, food for the Nanny."

"Okay stay on him." He called Nicky to see where he was. He was still on Frankie's tail. They decided it was time to act quickly to tie up loose ends in order to get the child home. Sitting curbside, Nicky who now had Giovanni's cell phone texted Frankie. *"This is Giovanni, Boss just paid me. We need to meet, so I can give you your money and your new set of identification and other credentials. I also have the location of the other safe house out of town. Meet me around the corner. I'm in a black sedan which you will use to skip town."* Nicky watched as Frankie came down the steps of his place. He had on a hat and dark shades. As he turned the corner Nicky fired on him from his vehicle using a silencer. No witnesses. Again, the dark van pulled alongside Frankie and his body was hoisted up into the van.

Lastly, it was time to move in on Lenny. They had to be sure the baby was still inside the hotel. They waited until nightfall. Nicky texted Lenny's burner from Frankie's phone with the same message they'd sent to Giovanni. He then used Giovanni's phone sending him a message that he had already received his money, and they all needed to keep their mouths closed about the baby and Delilah. In the staged text, he wished them both luck and said his goodbyes. When Lenny saw the messages, he was relieved. He thought they were still alive. He expected to receive his money so he could leave town, just as he thought they had done. He was ready to get rid of the baby so that he could move on with his life. He quickly responded to the text,

"What took you so long? I'm sick of this kid. She's crying at all times of the day and night. The old bitch can't seem to keep her quiet. Boss said not to hurt the baby, but I'm tempted to drop her and that bitch in the Hudson."

"I'm on my way now," was the message he received. Once Lenny received the text to step outside to pick up his money, he placed zip ties on Clara and placed duct tape on her mouth so he could step outside and get his pay. He walked outside the hotel and anxiously waited in the parking lot. He walked a little way down the sidewalk and slightly outside the hotel parking lot. He noticed the dark-colored van with headlights blinking. The van pulled alongside him. He quickly hopped inside not knowing it was a set-up. A black pillowcase was placed over his head, and he was shot and killed. His body was pulled in the back with the other two men and was quickly whisked away. All three men were killed within two hours. Their bodies were taken to an

incinerator and disposed of, leaving no trace of their deaths.

Nicky disguised his voice and used Lenny's burner to call the hotel manager to report the missing child. "Jersey's Inn, how may I direct your call?"

"Hey there. I'd like to report a noise complaint. I can't help but notice there's a baby in room one-twelve and it's screaming at the top of its lungs. I've seen a man coming to and from the hotel. He looks suspicious. I think he has something to do with the missing Wilkes kid from Tennessee everybody's talking about. I hear there's a reward for whoever finds the child. Can you please check to see if it's the same baby?"

"Sure, I'll check. What's your name sir?" Click…..

Nicky ended the call, destroyed the cell phones then took the van to another location and destroyed it as well. They made a clean and untraceable getaway.

The manager checked the tapes and noticed that Clara and the baby had been taken into the room and hadn't come out for a few days. As he continued to watch the surveillance video, he only saw Lenny coming to and from the room. Suspicious, he called the police. He showed them the video footage. After the police conducted their investigation, they called the room, but Clara didn't answer. Knowing she had gone inside and never came out, they wanted to go inside immediately. The police were afraid that if they forced their way inside, she would possibly harm the child. The manager quietly used his master key to open the door. Clara thought it was Lenny coming inside. After police gained entry into the room, they noticed Clara lying on the bed, bound and gagged, with the baby lying next to her. The baby was taken away, and Clara was quickly arrested.

The baby was taken to the hospital to be checked. Once Peyton heard about her child, she let out a loud cry. Her feet couldn't move fast enough. They were immediately flown to New York, where they were united with their baby. The police escorted their vehicle to the hospital. Peyton could hardly wait for the car to stop before she jumped out. She ran towards the entry doors of the hospital with Gil directly on her trail. The female officer stood in the waiting area of the emergency room. She was waiting to escort her to the examination room where their child was being cared for. She noticed a white female nurse holding Grace and singing to her. Peyton cried as she reached for her. "My baby! Thank you, God!" she exclaimed while kissing Grace. Grace had been cleaned and was wearing a fresh pamper and a hospital tee shirt. She was loosely wrapped in a blanket. Her clothing had been taken as evidence. Peyton looked her baby over from head to toe. Grace flashed her unmistakable smile when she saw her parents. She appeared as though the kidnapping had never fazed her. Gil held them both in his arms. Tears flowed heavily as they consoled each other and comforted their child. The family was allowed a few moments to reunite with their child. Afterwards, they were briefed on what they found.

As word poured in about the baby's safe return, the media began to cover the story nationwide. Clara was taken to the hospital to be checked out; once it was determined that she was okay, she was taken to headquarters for thorough questioning. While she tried playing the victim, citing her being found bound and gagged, authorities knew she was heavily involved in the kidnapping. Her phone records indicated that she had direct contact with the kidnappers up until they all ditched their phones. She was also seen driving away with the child in Peyton's car. Once she realized her crime was discovered, she confessed to her involvement and cooperated with the authorities to help find Lenny. She had no way of knowing he was already dead. She was booked into jail and was awaiting extradition back to Tennessee. The payday she thought was due her came in the form of legal justice.

Dante Castellucci cooperated with the FBI, and his attorney allowed him to be questioned by the media. He knew he could stand up to any scrutiny so long as he didn't have to take a polygraph test. He appeared open and honest. Everyone felt he was being truthful and was an unsuspecting victim of his wife's crime. Not even his attorney knew the truth. All evidence was destroyed, leaving absolutely no sign of Dante Castellucci's involvement. Actually, he was in attendance at an important business meeting in Washington D.C. with several politicians while the murders took place. He remained there until the baby's discovery. He only flew in as a public show after the baby had been returned to her family

Unaware that Delilah's henchmen were already deceased, authorities assumed they were still on the run. They continued looking for them.

Authorities were relieved they were able to reunite Grace with her parents, and Samuel Banks was alive and resting with his family.

CHAPTER NINE

It was Saturday evening. Delilah's loved ones were gathered at the cemetery. Dante stood before the champagne-colored casket containing the body of his beloved wife. Next to him was his mother-in-law, Sophia. She stood with her head down, sobbing into a silk handkerchief. Dante placed his arm around her, and he sobbed. He was truly heartbroken. He thought he would go before her. His pain was deep and confusing as he still felt responsible for neglecting her in her time of need. The guilt ate away at him as he continued staring at the casket. He barely heard a word as the minister read from the bible. He longed for the day and the memorial service to be over so he could take time away to grieve in private. There had been so many questions from the public, and he did as much as he could to resolve the subject. His attorney asked the public to allow the family to grieve in peace, and he would no longer conduct any more interviews concerning the matter. Although many stories on the kidnappings would remain, and more would be written for years to come, for the most part, it was made clear that all families involved wanted to go back to living a normal life as before.

Delilah had a large family back in Italy, but only a few were in attendance at Dante's request. They had their own memorial service in her honor in their family's native land.

There were a few Hollywood celebrities and filmmakers of her hit movies who came to pay their respects. Also, in attendance were Lucio, Tommy, and Dante's three cousins. They stood in the second row behind Dante and Sophia. Seeing the pain on Dante's face, they felt bad for him. At the end of the service, each mourner sprinkled dirt on the casket. Everyone began to walk away, leaving Dante and Sophia standing alone. His friends looked on with pity. The media was staked out, but they were respectful and kept their distance.

Sophia placed her head on Dante's chest. "She was all I had. Now my life is over."

"I'm so sorry, Mama Sophia. She was my world. I don't know what I'm going to do without her. The only thing left for us to do now is to grieve and try to heal. Just because she's gone doesn't mean I'm letting you out of my life. I'm going to take care of you. It's what I want to do because you're family. Besides, she would want that."

"Oh, you don't have to trouble yourself with me. I'll make it. I know you're a busy man. You still have some life left in you. You should get about it. Find someone else to love. You still have time."

"Mama Sophia, I don't even want to think about that now. I don't think I'll ever find someone who'll make me feel like my dear Delilah. She was one of a kind, for sure. As far as you're concerned, you don't have anything else to worry about. As I said, I will make sure you're cared for and protected. First, I will release all property and royalties for her work and sign it over to you. Any property and rights owned by your daughter will be released to you at your request. My company will still be overseeing all said properties, images, and works. I know it's not about the money with you, but I'm sure you'll enjoy knowing you have some control over when, where, and how Delilah's work can be used and distributed. If you need anything, and I do mean anything, you had better not hesitate to let me know. I must make sure you're okay. You may not have birthed me, but I'm still your son, and I love you."

He continued holding her. "I love you too son," she said as she gently pulled away to wipe her tears."

"Are you ready to leave, or do you still need some time? Dante asked.

"I'm ready," she said. They said their last goodbye and she kissed the casket. She got her purse from the chair. Dante stood with his arm slightly bent so she could place her arm in his. They slowly walked back to the waiting limousine. They gathered for the repass and spent time with family and friends. Afterwards, Dante went to his penthouse, while Sophia was taken to her home.

When he arrived, he decided to go through his mail. After thumbing through a few letters and other cards, he found one, in particular, that was given to him. He read it, and he knew he wanted to open this one. It was from Peyton Wilkes. He carefully opened it and began to read.

"Dearest Mr. Dante Castellucci, I heard about the death of your lovely wife. I know your heart must be aching at such a great loss. Although I have mixed feelings, I am sure of this; I would never wish to harm anyone. I don't consider Mrs. Castellucci an enemy—only a desperate woman who was at her wit's end and criminally handled

her issues. I'm truly sorry for your loss because I believe otherwise; she was a great person who may have brought joy to many.

I want to thank you from the bottom of my heart for being instrumental in bringing our daughter home. I trusted you when you told me not to worry, and in my heart, I knew you would do everything within your power to help reunite us with our child. You'll never admit this or accept it was your hand that helped bring about this change. I personally thank you, and I know you had nothing to do with the kidnapping of my daughter, or our beloved Mr. Sam. It is by God's grace and mercy that we were able to bring them both home safely. Thank you again for reassuring us that we would never be bothered in this way again, and we accept your sincere apology.

I consider you a friend, and I will keep you in my prayers. P.S. Thank you for the generous financial gift for baby Grace. Although we hadn't sought monetary damages, as we were only interested in her safe return, we are pleased that you sought to make things right by doing so. Again, thank you, and God bless. Peyton Wilkes."

Dante placed the letter back in the envelope. With a slight smile, he tried picturing the smile on Peyton's face. He was happy for her and the family. Dante, wanting to get ahead of any possible lawsuits concerning his wife's crimes, sent the Wilkes family a large payment for Delilah's behavior. He did the same for Samuel Banks, which made him an even wealthier man. Each of Gil's employees at the clinic was compensated as well. Everyone who had been negatively affected by his wife's actions was compensated financially. The payout was so huge that nobody sought legal action against the Castellucci organization. Dante backed out of the MSP deal. Although he was cleared of any involvement, he decided to take it easy until the noise died down. The kidnapping had taken its toll on him, and he was afraid it would affect his business. He didn't want to appear to aggressively pursue this particular business venture, in light of the recent events. He would try again in the future but for now, he wanted to live a quiet, more reserved life.

One Year later

Gil had moved Samuel into his medical condo temporarily so that he could be cared for around the clock. After a three-month stay, he began rehabilitation. He made a wonderful recovery; however, he used a walking cane from time to time. Silvia moved him into her home as her live-in boyfriend. They were making plans to build a home together and rent Samuel's home.

Samuel was surrounded by his children, who had come for a visit. It was nearing time for them to leave. They were still uneasy about what happened to their father. They feared losing him. Every chance they got, they would try to convince him to move near them. Samuel refused to go back to Louisiana with his children.

Silvia came into the room with coffee and snack packs she'd prepared for their flight back to New Orleans. She listened on as his daughter Pamela made one last plea,

"Daddy, are you sure we can't get you to move back with us? We just want you to be okay. You'll need someone to look after you, and we're worried about you. After all, the kidnappers are still on the loose."

"There's nothing to be worried about, baby," he said, taking his cup of coffee from the tray Silvia held out for him. "I'm not worried about those kidnappers. I'm sure they're on the run. The last person they want to see is me. I'm perfectly fine right where I am. Memphis is my home, and it will be until the day I die. I don't plan on that happening for a long time. I'm no coward. I'm not about to let fear run me off. Trouble could be anywhere. Who's to say if I move there, I'll be any safer?"

"But Daddy, you can identify them. What if they want to return and shut you up for good this time?"

"One, the police already know who they are, so without my testimony, they're still exposed; two, they would have to be fools to come after me now, and three, I'm not leaving home. I've made my peace with God. I want to enjoy the rest of my life, and I want to enjoy it with this beautiful lady right here. I have the right to be happy, and my quality of life is so much better now that I have Ms. Silvia in it. I don't want to move, and I never will. I love you, but you all need to come to terms with my decision. Trust that I know exactly what I want, and allow me to live my life in peace. I would never try and tell you how to live your lives. I can only give you sound advice, but in the end, the decision is yours. I've made mine, and you will respect it. Please don't ask again. It only causes stress when you do."

His daughter exhaled. She looked at her brothers and then back at her father.

"Okay, Daddy. I'm sorry for putting so much pressure on you. We can see that you're happy. Just promise me you'll take care of yourself."

"As you can see, I'm in great hands." He placed his hand on Silvia's knee who was now sitting beside him. "With the good Lord by my side, the support of my children, and my love, Silvia, I'll be okay. Not to mention, I have great friends who love me. I have everything I need right here in Memphis. With your portion of the Castellucci settlement, you guys are now well off. You don't have to work another day in your life if you so choose. Have fun, travel the world, and be free. In the meantime, Silvia and I will build our dream home. Our family home will be left to you to do as you please. I only pray you keep it in the family for your mother's sake. After all, it is your childhood home. There were a lotta great memories made there. Memories I would love to keep in the family. Perhaps one of you will make use of it. Silvia and I will live between here and her place until our new home is built. Now Pamela, Sam Jr., Elijah. I love you. With all these new ways for us to keep in touch, you'll hear from me often." They drank their coffee and chatted for a while. When the time came, they said their goodbyes and left.

CHAPTER TEN

It was nine in the morning at the local elementary school. Everyone was gathered in the gymnasium for a special assembly. It was a celebration for Samuel. The news media was there, and Kali Thompson, the original reporter of the kidnappings, covered the exclusive celebration. Since it was during the morning broadcast when they aired the news, the show was carried live. As everyone gathered, waiting for the celebration to begin, she spoke into the mic.

"Good morning, viewers; as we promised, we're live here at the Memphis elementary school, where a celebration is being held in honor of a well-known and beloved guy. His name is Samuel Banks. Mr. Banks has been through a lot over the past year. As you all may remember he was badly injured during the well-known Castellucci kidnapping. Mr. Banks is doing well. As you can tell by the crowd gathered behind me, he is well loved among these children, parents, and staff. Everyone is here including the city's mayor. We're going to take a quick break but when we come back, we'll share more."

Samuel and Silvia were seated behind the podium. Gil and Peyton sat in the front row in the audience. Baby Grace, who was now a walking toddler, sat in her mother's lap, drinking juice from a sippy cup as Gil watched on in protective mode.

After a few more minutes of everyone finding their seats, the program began. The principal took his place.

"Hello everyone. We're all gathered here today to honor a man who's like family to us here at the Memphis Elementary School. For many years he's volunteered at this school. Not only does he give of his time, but his generous financial donations have made it possible for many students who perhaps otherwise couldn't participate in certain programs due to their lack of funding, are now able to do so. His kindness and generosity have been instrumental in helping our youths learn the love of reading, and many books have been donated on his behalf. This has made a positive impact on not only our school but our community. Mr. Samuel Banks. I speak for all of us today when I say, we sincerely thank you; we love you, and we missed you when you were away. Welcome home."

There was loud applause from the audience as the principal stepped away from the mic to applaud Samuel. "Our city mayor is here, and he has a few words for you."

The mayor walked up and took his place. "Good morning, Memphis. It's a pleasure to be able to stand before you and partake in such a wonderful occasion to honor a great man. Samuel, you are the epitome of greatness. The kind of man that the people of Memphis can be proud of.

Your dedication to this city and its citizens, especially the youngest ones, has made a positive impact. You've changed many young lives. We want to say thank you from the bottom of our hearts for all you do in this community.

In honor of your dedication and your volunteering, the city of Memphis would like to honor you permanently. We're naming the new children's library after you. Also, the library in this elementary school will be renamed the Samuel R. Banks Library in your honor. This plaque is to be hung in this school to which you so lovingly gave of your time, love, and attention. Mr. Banks; please come forth."

Samuel stood to his feet proud and strong as the audience erupted in thunderous applause.

"We present this plaque to you and simply say thanks."

Samuel took his plaque. He and the mayor shook hands, and he stepped to the mic

"Thank you, mayor, Principal Jackson. I'd like to say thank you, to all of Grandpa Banks' family out there. I missed you. Grandpa Banks is back, and I'm ready for the new year. Also, if you don't mind, Grandpa Banks would like to introduce someone very special. Sweetheart, will you please come and join me?" he said speaking to Silvia.

Children I'd like to introduce you to Grandpa Banks' new helper. Her name is Grandma Silvia Banks. She will join me in marriage, and she will also be joining me in reading with you. I hope you will make her feel as welcome as you've made me."

He waited for the applause. Sweetheart, would you like to say something?"

"Thank you for that warm welcome. I was so excited when Grandpa Banks asked me to join him in one of his great passions. He truly loves you, children. I'm looking forward to meeting all of you and spending many great moments together." Silvia stepped back from the podium. Samuel took her hand and they both walked back to their seat.

"As they took their seats the lights were lowered. The mayor's liaison took the mic and said, this bust of Mr. Samuel Jackson will be installed at the new children's library in the coming weeks. The large black cloth that covered the statue, was quickly removed to reveal the perfect smile of Samuel. He enjoyed seeing an image of him. He'd be memorialized throughout the years. He was humbled.

After the ceremony, the school day began as usual. After all the teachers had escorted their children to their classes, Samuel and Silvia went to the kindergarten wing, where they'd been gathered together in the library for a special storytime. Samuel narrated just like old times, and Silvia joined him in the reading. Peyton and Gil were in the library as well with baby Grace. After story time, they left the elementary school and went out for breakfast.

Dante Castellucci went on to live his life and found love again. This time she was more his age. He still has yet to marry her. Samuel didn't want to stop working with the Wilkes family, but Gil insisted that he retire.

Although he and Silvia were no longer employed by the family, they were a constant presence in the home. Silvia stayed on briefly to help familiarize the new employees with their duties. Peyton never hired another nanny for the baby.

Gil's practice continued to flourish. He took on more physicians and opened several more clinics in the South. Gil, his father, Peyton's dad, and Sam continue their golf tradition still playing for pennies.

About The Author

Karen Coleman is an Arkansas native. She enjoys writing exciting and dramatic stories. A phenomenal author with a distinctive style, she has demonstrated a sensational talent for steering her readers through every line and page with eager anticipation.

Karen has published several novels in various genres. Readers have described her novels as riveting, fast-paced, and thrilling. Her teen novels are insightful and empowering. As a mentor who has worked with teens for many years, Karen understands the social challenges they face, and she skillfully addresses those topics with a finesse that lends excitement, adventure, and encouragement.

A self-proclaimed writer of fiction with an element of truth, Karen began penning her thoughts as a hobby. After many years of writing and encouragement from those around her, she began writing on a more intense level, eventually turning out several wonderful novels. She offers something for almost every reader, from her adult crime series to her teen books, there's something to be enjoyed by all. Her literary works have garnered much fanfare and have not only been enjoyed by her many readers; she's highly celebrated among her writing peers. Her books are meant to inspire, uplift, and entertain, leaving her audience asking for more.

Karen is also a playwright, actor, and former city council member. She's the mother of four and a Glam-ma of thirteen and counting. Her grandchildren affectionately call her Nana. She's also the proud mom of two rambunctious miniature schnauzers. When not writing or spoiling her grandbabies, she spends her time crafting, fishing, or enjoying a great barbecue.

www.ingramcontent.com/pod-product-compliance
Lightning Source LLC
Chambersburg PA
CBHW020742250626
47155CB00003B/871